Whiskey Eyes

Simon Nyok

Whiskey Eyes

Ken Rivard

Black Moss Press
2004

National Library of Canada Cataloguing in Publication

Rivard, Ken, 1947-
    Whiskey eyes / Ken Rivard.

Fiction.
ISBN 0-88753-391-4

    I. Title.

PS8585.I8763W44 2004   C811'.54   C2004-901864-7

Published by Black Moss Press at 2450 Byng Road, Windsor,
Ontario N8W 3E8. Black Moss books are distributed in
Canada and the U.S. by Firefly Books.

Black Moss would like to acknowledge the generous support
of the Canada Council and the Ontario Arts Council for their
publishing programs.

ONTARIO ARTS COUNCIL
CONSEIL DES ARTS DE L'ONTARIO

Le Conseil des Arts | The Canada Council
du Canada | for the Arts

For Micheline, Annie, Melissa and H.P.

OTHER BOOKS BY KEN RIVARD:

KISS ME DOWN TO SIZE (poetry, 1983).

FRANKIE'S DESIRES (poetry, 1987).

IF SHE COULD TAKE ALL THESE MEN (short fiction, 1995) – Finalist for The Writers Guild Of Alberta, Howard O'Hagan, 1996, Best Short Fiction Book Award.

MOM, THE SCHOOL FLOODED (children's picture book, 1996).

SKIN TESTS (short fiction, 2000) – Finalist for The Writers Guild Of Alberta, Howard O'Hagan, 2001, Best Short Fiction Book Award and Finalist for The City of Calgary, 2001, W.O. Mitchell Book Prize.

BOTTLE TALK (short fiction, 2002) – Finalist for The Writers Guild of Alberta, Howard O'Hagan, 2003, Best Short Fiction Book Award.

Acknowledgements

Several portions in this book have appeared in earlier forms in (on) the following: *ANTIGONISH REVIEW, ARC, ARIEL, BOTTLE TALK* (Black Moss Press, 2002), *CANADIAN LITERA-TURE, CBC RADIO, DANDELION, EVENT, FIDDLEHEAD, OUR FATHERS* (Poetry and Prose Anthology, Rowan Books, 1995), *PRAIRIE JOURNAL OF CANADIAN LITERATURE, PRISM, QUAR-RY, SANSCRIT* and *WHETSTONE*.

Special thanks to Byrna Barclay and her sharp-eyed, editorial suggestions.

The Marx Brothers quotes are from *GROUCHO* by Stefan Kanfer, copyright © 2000. Used by permission of Alfred A. Knopf, a division of Random House Inc.

Excerpt from ALIAS GRACE by Margaret Atwood is used by permission, McClelland & Stewart, Inc., The Canadian Publishers.

"*Gone mad* is what they say, and sometimes *Run mad,* as if mad is a direction, like west; as if mad is a different house you could step into, or a separate country entirely. But when you go mad you don't go any other place, you stay where you are. And somebody else comes in."

Alias Grace by Margaret Atwood

SIX-MONTH BENDER

"*ROUND UP THE PARTY ANIMALS! ROUND UP THE PARTY ANIMALS!*" says the tall, craggy-faced woman on TV who looks like she could talk herself out of her skin at any moment. Animals. Wolves. I ignore the ones inside my own heart and head, who know my nights, wild with fury. Crafty, cruel, carnivorous animals protecting themselves from the simplicity of no love.

"Try harder," I tell myself but the beasts, all wearing party hats, circle for the kill.

Picking up the remote, I press the MUTE button on TV and phone Montreal.

Think and drive! Think and drive!

"Your mother and I want a place close to yours," he says.

Designated driver. Designated driver.

"I know, J.L.." My father likes to be called J.L.. He once told us that Jonathan Louis sounded like the name of a rich man and that he certainly wasn't one of those.

"I've been looking around, J.L.," I say.

"After we've been in Calgary a year we'll move into a place where your mother and I don't have to cook or clean, like maybe a Senior Citizens Lodge. I've had to do everything since your mother was diagnosed last summer."

According to the doctor, it was a lot more complicated than just cataracts. Something about glaucoma, the fluid in her eyeball not draining properly and pressure in the eyeball building up. There is possible damage to the optic nerve, which connects the eye with the sight center of the brain. The doctor called it 'the sneak thief of sight' and said she may be too old to risk surgery.

"Now I have to do it all for both of us. And you know how Hazel was, even when she could see well."

It's so quiet I can hear the maws of a thousand wolves vibrating from Calgary to Montreal.

Don't be caught drinking and driving. Don't be caught drinking and driving.

"Can we just move in with you?" he asks. I knew he would.

"Ah, come on J.L., you've got to be joking. Aren't you?"

I've been weaned on J.L.'s teasing, years of it dished out at the supper table. I used to choke while laughing. He worked as a traffic clerk for the Canadian Pacific Railway, the C.P.R., and he mimicked his co-workers, particularly the ones who took themselves too seriously, saying: "Now, you try this face on." Some of the faces he aped were the accountant in the shiny brown suit. Then there was the receptionist who spent hours in the sun, the vice-president who talked too fast, smoked Cuban cigars and always had a full file folder growing out of his armpit. After, the office boy weaseling from desk to desk; and that salesman who whispered dirty jokes and used his empty coffee mug to emphasize a punch line.

"I'm serious, Mark," my father says.

"I've heard it never ever works," I say. "Parents living with their kids."

"We won't get in the way." After all, we have an extra room. I'll set up separate beds and dressers. Time to renew, reach out one more time. Extend.

"I'll have to talk this over with everyone."

CHECKSTOP! CHECKSTOP!

I hang up the phone and pace back and forth in front of the silent six o'clock news.

• • •

Pauline, Sarah and Marie come downstairs with slow, measured footsteps.

"We don't have much choice," Pauline says. Her brown eyes belong to an owl perched on the last tree branch in a Brazilian rain forest. Eyes unsure as to why they store up strength. Pauline is cautious, but calm, as if she were building a wall of protection around our discussion. "Your parents cannot take care of themselves anymore. They're your parents, Mark, but we're your family too and the idea of them moving in worries me, but what else can we do?" she says.

Energetic Sarah, who has a heart the size of a house, and who will please the world before she takes care of herself, just flashes her huge-eyed smile and says: "We'll do what we can, Dad." She's the optimist of the family, with arms big enough to embrace us all at the same time. "I've always wondered though, is Grandpa afraid of Grandma?" she asks.

Marie, who will often send us tumbling to the floor with her humor, has nothing funny to say. She is silent, rolls her chocolate-brown eyes towards the ceiling, her breathing unsure, her punch lines put on hold. "I have a hard time trusting Granny, even when she isn't drinking," Marie finally asks. "And how come the skin on her face looks thicker every time we see her?"

"Let's try it anyhow," I say working the carpet with my toe.

Then I phone my brother. "Just so it's very clear, Jimmy, if it doesn't work, we talk and if the talking doesn't work, they have to move out, maybe even to your house. I'll tell J.L. too."

"Whatever works. One day at a time," says Jimmy, sounding like a boy angel in a man's body, born with perpetual but equal amounts of both tenderness and wisdom.

Have I been drinking tonight? Have I?

• • •

I'll go out of my mind!
I have my own family to take care of.

I'll need my own space.
I'll want to move out of my own house.
Little things will get to me.
I'll begin to hate the way my parents breathe, eat, move, talk,
sit, sneeze, cough, even fight.
I'll have to become their parents.
My mother has been tying my brain in knots for as long as
I can remember.
They'll expect too much of my time.
Can't I get them their own place?
My parents can't care for themselves anymore.
Surgery.
Blindness.
Fear.
Hostility is usually a smokescreen for fear.
Me, I'm not afraid.
Try to put myself in their shoes.
Sure, that shouldn't be too hard.
I'll use my mistakes for fertilizer in my garden.

• • •

They don't qualify for a provincially-subsidized senior's lodge. Most places require at least six months residency in the province. They are alone, floating near the borders of neglect, fed up, and scared in Montreal. Hazel dusts the furniture always in her dark. Groping. Knocking. Muttering. J.L. leaves her alone at least three times a week and escapes to Tim Horton's for his chicken salad sandwich. "Just going for some fresh air," he tells Hazel. Today, he brings back a chicken salad sandwich for Hazel for the first time. She says: "You're such a good husband, J.L.. Really." And J.L. smiles his Boy Scout smile and figures he could now get away with one extra trip a week to Tim Horton's, J.L.'s doughnut heaven.

• • •

We're supposed to be packing for our move to Calgary. Now I have to enter the hospital for surgery. The knife. Prostate surgery. Cancer. The big "C". Damn! Who will take care of ME? Who will take care of ME? Hazel can barely see now. But I need her. I need her. They'll cut me up. Take the cancer out. Throw it away. So they say. I'll have to rest. Get better. Mark and Jimmy are so far away. Twenty-three hundred miles away. Calgary is on the other side of the world! Why didn't they move to Ottawa or Toronto, anywhere closer to Montreal. We need to pack. We need to pack. No, I need to live. Put the packing on hold. Maybe Mark and Jimmy will fly into town to visit me in the hospital. Mark: smart, strong. Jimmy: smart, always smart, his brain is a book, like you, Tim Horton. Are you in Calgary, too? Tim, can you spare a few hours away from the doughnuts and coffee? You've got the muscle to help me pack. All those years playing on the blue line for the Toronto Maple Leafs and the Buffalo Sabers. Did I miss any team, Tim? Did I? Sorry. Everyone says you died in a car accident. Show me it's not true, Tim. Come and visit me in the hospital. That'll show everyone you're still alive. We'll gobble down a couple of those chocolate-glazed doughnuts with your coffee. Best in the world. Did your dad ever have Cancer, Tim? What's that you say? He had prostate Cancer, like me. And he's still alive? Thanks, Tim, the packing can wait. Calgary can wait. Mark and Jimmy can wait. I love the smell of your famous coffee. Helps me taste and smell.

Memory triggers. Yes, I do remember when I thought Cancer only happened to people in movies and on TV.

• • •

Back in Calgary, I try my twin daughters' old beds and dressers in each of the two rooms downstairs. The smaller room might be suitable for my office, and a private place of my own to write. Freezer, books, bookshelves, filing cabinet, computer, desk, cot, ironing board, chairs. I move them all into the smaller room. For a few hours I try on this arrangement like a new shirt but the room is too small. I move everything back. My parents will simply have to use the smaller of the two rooms. Everything looks good. Duty. Order. I imagine the walls covered with Hazel's holy pictures: St. Jude, St. Joseph, The Virgin Mary. On her bureau is a statue of St. Anthony, the saint who finds the lost. The statue is missing its right index finger and its head is chipped above both unseeing eyes. "My Saint Anthony has been through a lot," my mother says. I see J.L.'s C.P.R. APPRECIATION PLAQUE hanging in the corner directly above his bed. THANKS FROM ALL THE GUYS IN THE OFFICE. Piled high on his dresser are J.L.'s baseball books, mostly about pitchers like Hoyt Wilheim and Phil Niekro. Knuckleballers. Slow pitching, without spin, thrown with the first knuckles, or the nails, of the middle two or three fingers pressed against the ball, like a claw. You never know how the ball will come at the hitter, like my mother going at my father. Baseball once again. I hear J.L. listening to the Montreal Expos on his radio as they play an opponent away from Montreal and cursing whenever he's forced to watch the nationally televised game featuring the Toronto Blue Jays. I hear him joking about baseball and his missing testicles: "Two balls and I can even get a walk!"

I hear Hazel praying the ears off her favorite statue.

● ● ●

No more testicles but I can still think about sex. They didn't take my brain out. I remember a couple of years ago when Mark and I were driving back to his place after watching that movie called ON GOLDEN POND. I told him it was crucial that I have sex with his mother once a week. He laughed so hard that he nearly fell out of his car right there on the Deerfoot Trail Expressway. Well, forget I ever said that, Mark, because now I'll have to have sex inside my head. Try on this face, Mark. Try on this face. Oh, I love telling each visitor I had prostate Cancer and that I still might have some bad cells left. My eyes water up. My voice is breaking. Can you hear me? Can you hear me? When Mark was born, I threw my fedora hat up in the air and danced down the hospital corridor. My first son!

The nurses thought I was nuts. I'm in the same hospital now to have my testicles taken out. They say nothing happens by accident. I'll have to take it easy at home for a few days then get the packing started. A neighbour said she'd drop in at least twice a day. Don't worry boys, the neighbour will keep an eye on us. Shouldn't be for long. We're still coming to Calgary to be near you. What's that? The ceiling lights in my hospital room— they brighten, darken and brighten again. Who is now playing with my switch? Must be St. Mary. That mother.

• • •

It's Saturday morning and my father is again on the phone worrying at me, wearing the beard off his face. I can hear him scratching his stubble. Scratching. Scratching. He needs to discuss his plane tickets, his flight, especially the departure date. I remind him that my sister-in-law will take care of everything. "She's got all the information, Dad. She works for Canadian Airlines."

"I'm not sure. You know, I've been living here in Montreal for nearly eighty years. I haven't flown often. Never been anywhere much."

"Relax," I say. "I'll see what I can do."

Imagine his fear. Whenever he is faced with a big decision or conflict, J.L. drops his head, flings his hands at a wall and slaps his back, as if he were trying to rid himself of ants scurrying up and down his spine. My father hates to face up to anything unpleasant. He'd rather be wandering through one of his sky meadows, living in his better worlds.

Minutes later I'm on the phone with Jimmy.

"I've told Dad twice we'll take care of all travel arrangements," I say.

"Just relax," Jimmy says.

I *AM* relaxed. It's the roundabout way information is relayed between members of my family. Bleached. Bent. Mixed. Twisted. Straightened out with the word RELAX. Perhaps, I make myself too responsible for all the messages.

"But Dad's worried, Jimmy! Think about it. They are making such a big move. Mom is nearly seventy-nine and almost totally blind."

"I'll call him," my brother says. "Maybe get him to calm down."

"Remember, when we visited J.L. in the hospital and then brought him home. I started packing one of their closets and Hazel went crazy thinking I was not doing it right. She kept saying, 'Get out of my stuff! Get out of my stuff!' She sure knew where to find her whiskey that day. Anyhow, they've hired movers. Even though you offered to go get them and bring them to Calgary, J.L. and Hazel insist on coming on their own. They're now only a plane trip away."

We both laugh with a different father face. I do Groucho Marx, my father's hero, leaning forward with a loose-limbed lope around the room that makes me look like a robot trying to run away from a candy store after stealing a chocolate bar. I leer, flick my cigar, and with raised eyebrows, I order everyone to pack a hundred boxes as soon as possible and to jump into the boxes before closing the lids.

One of the helpers, the one with an ego the size of a moving van, is not happy: "I'm too smart to be packing boxes. I know what really makes people attractive. Some people say it's what's upstairs that counts," he says.

"I have something upstairs. My upstairs maid. And that's not easy, because I only have a one-story house. And the one story you're not going to hear is about my upstairs maid," I say. We have both seen the same movie.

Another helper, a woman with ten children says: "I'm much too busy to be packing boxes."

"Why did you have so many children? Ten kids, that's a

20

huge responsibility and an even bigger burden," I say.

"Well, because I adore my children, Groucho, and I think that's our purpose here on earth and I adore my husband," she says.

"I adore my cigar too, but I take it out of my mouth once in a while."

Jimmy pretends he's Harpo, mute, wide-eyed, face of a silent mapmaker, honking his honk and chasing a woman between empty boxes. We both stop and I swear I feel my father's comedy skin on me taking a bow for having trained Jimmy and me so well.

We direct the movers to pack everything in sight, including our zaniness.

A mover in coveralls offers to buy us plane tickets for anywhere.

• • •

When I hang up the phone I still hear my father. As usual he is having problems saying "no" to a salesman, as if he were afraid to disappoint him.

"All you have to do is convince ten people to display or buy this set of silverware in their homes."

"Just ten."

"Yes Sir."

"Then what?"

"You get to keep your silverware set. For free."

"How much time do I have to find these ten people?"

"Thirty days."

"What if I can't do it?"

"Then you have to pay for the silverware."

"Shouldn't be a problem", J.L. says.

My father signs a contract and discovers that each of his ten people has to get ten people and so on and so on – like a pyramid scam.

Not one uncle, aunt, neighbor or friend wants to display or buy the silverware. J.L. is stuck. And on the twenty-ninth day my mother wants to stab him with each and every silver knife.

"I told you not to do that," I hear Hazel growl. "Now we pay. Now we pay. We always pay."

"Yea, Yea. Yea," my father says, the insects now frozen in the middle of his back.

Later I will phone my parents and ask again if they will let me worry for them.

• • •

My mother drops the phone seconds after I call with an offer to take over all of hers and J.L.'s worries. "Sorry, Mark. It's hard to keep a grip on the phone. Must be my arthritis or indigestion."

"Don't worry, Mom. I'll take care of things."

Then the silence, the shutting out, the welling up of feelings, as if thinking had become dangerous for me. All my life, Hazel's had an ache or a pain, she begs for attention, like a girl who cries wolf. She has taught me to be deaf. Her words hang from a clothesline that cuts the sky in half. One part of her is an alcoholic with emotions running wild. The other half is sober with feelings tempered by rational thought.

– Get those creatures out of my bed! Now! Hazel yells at J.L..

– There are no creatures here, Hazel. Look again, he says.

– No, I can see them. Right there!

– See, Hazel, I'm pulling the blankets and sheets down. You had too much to drink again.

– No! No! No! Strip the bed!

– Okay, Hazel. Anything to get some sleep.

– Can't you see them J.L.? There, under the mattress.

– Look, Hazel. I'm lifting the mattress up. There's nothing there. Let's get to bed.

– Please, J.L., check again, under the bed. They're talking to me. I know they're there. Please.

– Alright, Hazel. Watch. I'm moving the whole bed over to the window.

– Be careful, they'll slide in through the window, under the door. They know I want to get some sleep. They scare me. Close the window, the door. Quick!

– Sure, Hazel. Sure. Before they make us both crazy.

"Mom, tell Dad I phoned and that all your worries are now in my hands."

"Ah, that's my son, the strong one. I always said you could do anything. Anything!"

• • •

We carry their suitcases in and they seem heavier than at the airport, luggage as silent as tombs belonging to people in deep thoughts, none of them revealed. Yet.

"Open that brown one, Mark'" my mother says.

"Let's get you settled first, Mom."

"Plenty of time for that. Open that brown suitcase. Now please!"

"What's in there, Hazel?" I ask, suspicious by habit.

"It's been a long trip. It will help me sleep tonight."

"Isn't it a little early?" my father says.

"Relax, J.L.. You can go to sleep whenever you want."

I open her suitcase and find five small bottles of rye lined up, like soldiers, under her sweaters and socks.

"I'll have a rye and water. You know how I take it, Mark."

"Listen, Hazel and listen good! You know I quit drinking a few years ago. Get Dad to make it for you."

"Will somebody, anybody, please pour me a drink?"

"Get your own," J.L. and I say at exactly the same time; my father and I have been practicing the words for years. We've tried everything to get Hazel to stop drinking: Throwing away the booze. Councellors. Therapy. Priests. Ministers. Detox Centers. Those meetings.

Then Pauline and I bring the other suitcases downstairs to my parents' bedroom. My father follows us downstairs together with my daughters, Marie and Sarah. We unpack as much as we can and head back upstairs. Then we see it. My mother's brown suitcase is open on the kitchen floor. Clothes are tossed everywhere. Hazel has managed to open one of her small bottles, and is fumbling from cupboard to cupboard, searching for a glass. The kitchen floor and counter are littered with pots, pans, plates, cups, cereal boxes, salt, ketchup, knives, forks and spoons. Some of the plates and cups are broken and the floor near the stove has become crunchy to a footfall.

"You people know I'm just about totally blind and now I have to grope around like a beggar to find a glass! Ah, here's one." My mother finds a dirty glass with a finger of milk still in it. She half-fills it with whiskey, turns on the hot instead of the cold water tap, fills her glass, and takes a sip.

"BLAH! This drink tastes warm and milky. Where do you keep your ice, Mark? Come on now, where do you keep your ice? You know what happens when you keep your mother waiting."

Pauline cleans up the mess and looks at everyone as if to say, 'how can anyone leave Hazel alone to drink?' We all rise at the same time from our kitchen chairs, hearts thumping like different-sized drums at the end of a song, and leave for our rooms.

● ● ●

In our bedroom downstairs, there is a statue of St. Anthony, an enormous framed picture of Jesus Christ and a hand-carved wooden replica of the Twelve Stations Of The Cross. They are steps. Up to God. They each remind me that they're only symbols; God knows I need to see something to get to Him. I cannot walk up invisible steps. I just can't be simple like Mark, on his knees in the morning, saying "please" and "thank you" at night. Now that I'm nearly blind, I see the steps behind my eyes. My fingers trace the face and beard of Christ and feel His tears, the scars from the thorns. My nostrils open wider when

I smell His blood. I lift one of my fingers to my lips, tasting the salt from His sweat. I blow dust off His face. Next, I pick up the St. Anthony statue, rub its chest and bring it close to my own heart. Hazel heart to statue heart. "I'm sorry for the damage to your head," I say, referring to the two chips above St. Anthony's eyes. Must have happened during the move. "You work so hard for my family. You really do. Wish I could see you." And my fingertips work their way down, over the statue's gown and sandal feet, mapping for more chips or cracks. Then, I trace over each of the Twelve Stations Of The Cross. I'll take His place. Nobody will notice! I'll even wear leather sandals, a simple robe: white, soiled, ripped, and worn. Finally, the world will track my suffering, thorn by thorn. I am ready for the nails. I test the blindness of my faith. Someone from far away tells me to get off the cross because the world needs the wood.

• • •

My eyeballs are filling with water.
No pain.
No swelling.
No blurred vision.
No redness.
The glaucoma happened so slow, so ... fast.
My eyeballs are blocked with fluid.
Nowhere for the fluid to go.
Where's my rye?
Fill me.
Fill me.
I can see clearly now.
Better than the song.
Then to the sink or toilet.
Those big white telephones.
There's always a call from me to me.
I vomit from the tips of my toes.

I vow to stop drinking tomorrow.
Again. Again.
I imagine my eyeballs filled with booze.
I drink from one eye at a time, each to each, and forever.

• • •

J.L. and Hazel have paid to have half of their possessions moved here thinking I might be able to use some but there is not enough room here. Most of what they brought will be donated to the Salvation Army, like leftover love. The moving truck unloads everything into the garage. Boxes. Boxes. Old furniture. Clothes in suitcases and old trunks. We spend the next day sorting through boxes, my mother needing to be told what each item is and my father not caring as long as his TV for baseball games is moved in first. Boxes. Boxes. Sorting. When going through one box, Pauline finds J.L.'s green, tin strongbox with the steel handle. My mother always seemed to ignore this green box and once said that it was J.L.'s "man place" to keep important papers. The lid flips open after Pauline lays the box down and a yellow sheet of paper slides to the floor. It's a letter. Pauline reads the short letter to me in her usual hushed and tactful voice:

30 June, 1947

DEAR JOHNNY,

Do you have any idea how long it has been since we made love? Do you? I know you are just trying to be decent to your wife because your baby is due any day now. Must be about a week since we've been in each other's arms. I'm taking a big chance by dropping this note off at your office but I had to get it to you somehow. Fast. I hope your baby is a boy. I know how much you want a son. If it is a boy, I hope he is as gentle and easy-going as you are. If he's as handsome as you are, he'll stop women in their tracks. Please give me a call when it happens and if it's a boy. Another man like you is hard to find.

> *Love You Forever,*
> *Maureen*

Pauline has her hand at her mouth and her eyes are as big as billiard balls. She wants to know if Maureen is still alive, perhaps—or worse, still in my father's head. But being the protective person she is, Pauline thinks of using the letter to line the bottom of the first box earmarked for the Salvation Army. Instead she slips the letter back inside the steel box, as if she realizes the letter is not hers to dispose of in any way.

That night, after the shock, my hurt, my anger has dissipated. I giggle, slowly at first, and then shake our bed with my laughter. Then, Pauline and I imagine and describe J.L.'s secret lover in detail: taller than my mother, slimmer, maybe one green eye and one blue eye, a face made for teasing, wanting to love, easy to love, gentle as a new tulip bulb in my garden. We pretend to be secret lovers. We rehearse. Rehearse again. With her fingertips, Pauline writes MAUREEN, MAUREEN, MAUREEN all over my body.

● ● ●

The next morning, the sound of my father's cough wheezes up the vent in my bedroom. When he was a child, he was trapped in a fire, and he's been coughing ever since. I lie awake, with both eyes opened upstairs. J.L.'s coughs are punctuation marks around a silence begun long ago. On nights when she was drinking, one moment Hazel would say she loved him so, so much and with her next breath say he was as useless as a dog with no bark. Now I imagine my mother cleaning her ears under the blankets. My parents' voices are like puffs of dust seeking freedom from the vent.

– I just want to be near him.

– We are living in HIS house.
– He was never easy to love.
– He's the boss now.
Inside my head, I hear:

> Father: *Show me how to love you.*
> Mother: *Don't push us away.*

I've never been easy to love. My brother says I always seemed like an island, away from the rest of the family. And my body isn't home for my memories either. When I was six, a sixteen-year-old boy named Fritz down the street wanted me to play with him under a thick, green, woolen blanket in a field of grass as tall as I am. He pulled me under the blanket and his breathing filled the dark. His hands moved all over me and his face was too close to mine. Then he tried to force my head everywhere but I fought free from the woolen terror before anything happened. With my stomach lurching, I grabbed at the sunlight and took off. When I was close to home, I stopped at a bush for a split second, checked between my legs and ran inside the apartment. I told my mother what happened. "I'm so glad you told me," she saai. "Are you okay? Stay away from THAT BOY. Now, where's my rye?"

She didn't believe me.

She couldn't see.

The bruises.

Coughing is the only sound squeezed through the vent.

• • •

I keep my partial plate in a blue Tupperware cup sealed with a white rubber top. I still remember the color blue, that feeling, strong as a memory. I hold the cup to the light. The river is narrow, the raft large, pink and as yellow-white as a young sun. Someone is perched on a raft, and she looks like me. I'm wearing my white, 40's bathing suit and a bubble-gum colored bathing cap. My smile is as wide and perfect as the sun on the water. I may have been born on this raft, on this river, beneath the sun. Two men swim towards the raft. One is J.L.. The other man slices through the water with the grace and strength of a long distance swimmer. When I take the children to visit him he takes out a jar of coins and tells them to count them out, very carefully. They may keep them if the sum is correct. Then we disappear into the bedroom. Ice cubes chinking in glasses. So much laughter. Now, in the water, J.L. is far behind, struggling with his sidestroke. He always feared the water. I wave at both of them, not sure who I want to win. My lover cuts through the water, swimming past the raft, as if he does not know me and so keeps our affair a secret. Then, J.L. reaches and grabs onto the raft, hoists up gasping. "You're a real beauty," he says. I grin, looking past the raft, losing my breath. He looks too much like my now grown son.

• • •

The warm water of my bath invites me somewhere.

I just can't get used to being shut out in the dark.

People get up, walk out of the room and I speak to empty chairs.

Empty chairs. Empty rooms.

I wander. Wait. Plead.

Most people forget that I've only recently lost most of my sight. I hate it when Pauline, Mark or the girls suddenly return minutes later. They can't even apologize properly. Doesn't matter now, even here in my very own bathtub. I splash. I splash. Wash my eyes too.

  – Hazel, is that a choir girl in the bathtub?

  – J.L., that's you fooling around. Bet you're making one of your faces too.

  – I'm calling the newspapers to tell them there's a choir girl loose in the bathtub.

  – You're making me laugh too hard. Stop, will ya! I can't

wash myself properly. If I could, I'd throw this huge wet sponge at you.

– I can hear your laughing bounce off the walls, Hazel. That's my girl! Sing some kind of mother song or something.

– What do you want to hear, J.L.?

– Your pick, Hazel.

– Oh J.L., J.L. would you be a real Sweetie and drop a few ice cubes into a glass of rye for me please?

I sing "O COME ALL YE FAITHFUL". It's the middle of July, but who cares? My wet, wet arms slice through the bubbly water, chorus after chorus. I sing alto, tenor. Even a few base notes. My harmonies are perfect. One voice catches up to another. They wait in line to be washed. Clean.

• • •

My mother practices. Her arms protrude like divining rods used to find water. Hands slide along the kitchen counter. Feel for the toaster. Still warm. Still. Warm steel. Places the toaster back down on the counter. Her fingers reach over, to the bread. They poke. Plunge. Spongy bread. Whole wheat sponge. Then the stove, its four big steel eyes. The cupboards. Small, smooth wooden walls with handles. Open door. Close. Open. Close. Tea bags. Cup. Along the counter. A sudden drop into the sink. Taps. Steel. Up, over more counter. The warm walls of the refrigerator. Handle. Open. Beef tongue. She grabs a piece of meat and slaps it on a piece of whole wheat. The beef tongue hangs from the bread. Back at the table she slices her sandwich into uneven triangles. She seems not to care, and when I dab at the mayonnaise on her cheeks, then wipe her fingers with a napkin, she laughs.

"If I'm hungry enough, I'll find something to eat," she says. "Think I'll have another one."

"Why not?" I say.

"Too thick'" she says.

"Too sloppy," she says.

"Where's the mayonnaise?" she says.

Then Hazel stops mid-way to the table and seems to stare hard at us. "Hey, stop whispering and making all those faces, will ya. You're distracting me."

Then my mother waits, like a queen, for me to prepare her sandwich, her tea and three Digestive cookies for dessert.

• • •

One morning at Mark's, Hazel says she's taking her ears downstairs to listen to stories about the Federal Referendum on a radio talk-show. Why bother? I can tell her how it's all going to turn out. When it comes to politics, Hazel usually sees a politician as the central character in a nightmare, but today is different. Just GO Hazel so I can have some peace and quiet to read my Charlie Chaplin biography. But, here she comes, her white cane stabbing towards me. She says Quebec may really be ready to leave Canada. So what! I do my Charlie Chaplin routine, duck-walking around her in a circle, just far enough to miss the tip of her cane. Really, ready. Really, ready. Really, ready. She yells at me to stop: *I can't see you. I can't see you!* So I turn on some vaudeville piano on the stereo. Make faces of two people leaving each other. Laugh a hard, dry laugh. Hazel yells again: *I hear you, you bugger! Where are you ,J.L.? Where are you?* Her voice is a shriek that leaves its fingerprints in the air. *You're not going anywhere, so cut out the Charlie Chaplin routine!* But no, who knows who will die first? Death is my own brilliantly, black cane.

• • •

I can't find my favorite radio station. J.L.'s fingers trip over each other; finding and adjusting any dial drives him crazy. It's like zippers, I always tell him. He's had trouble with zippers for fifty years. Then he finds it: QR77. Quiet, easy music. Some light, light rock. Classical. Lots of talk, discussion with listeners. I feel like a child clapping her hands after receiving a gift. After J.L. pulls up the antenna and guides my fingers to it, he lets them slip down to the "ON / OFF" switch. I practice two or three times. A radio station of my own. Look at that announcer, he's wearing a blue silk shirt and black slacks. Snazzy. He must be anxious to finish the morning show. It's his daughter's birthday and a wrapped doll is at his elbow. Neil Diamond sings HAPPY BIRTHDAY to his daughter. Another happy birthday song comes from Anne Murray. I wish he'd lighten up and get on with the phone-in calls. Hello. Hello. I have a question for you. Is your daughter listening this morning? If you were behind my eyes, birthdays wouldn't matter. I remember when I was born. I need a drink. Where's that rye? I feel like green water turning black, sluggish. I resent everyone in this damn family. Mark hates me. He never wanted to sit on my knee.

I remember light. I can see it on the radio.

• • •

Somehow, tiny beads of water have trickled, like unwanted prayers, into my parents' bedroom downstairs. I stop the leak by pinning the eaves troughs closer to the edge of the roof with special aluminum nails and sleeves. But for days afterwards, Hazel gropes her way to the washroom, palms doing miniature pushups from wall to picture to wall to picture to door to doorknob and then the awkward clicking of the light switch. Always, her pant or pajama legs are rolled up, and I say: "Mom, the bathroom carpet is completely dry!" "You never know, Mark. You never know. What if company comes over all of a sudden? What if your house springs another leak?" Weeks pass by and Hazel is still walking around the house with rolled-up pants or pajamas. "Even my skin can be rolled up at the sleeves if need be," she says. And a few days later we have another severe rainstorm, as if the sky were trying to prove my mother right. We watch my mother bob back and forth closer to the living-room window so she can hear the rain. "SSSSHH!" Hazel says to nobody in particular. "Listen. The whole world is rolling up its pant legs." Then she disappears into the washroom. Seconds later, my mother is back in the room with only one pant leg rolled up. "I may be legally blind but I know what you're all thinking. No, I haven't forgotten one of my pant legs. A flood has two parts." Hazel sits by the window as if she were guarding the house. Three chairs, with us in them, stand at offending-looking angles to each other. "Can't you hear it? The house, it's groaning in distress." And Hazel slowly rolls up her second pant leg, as if her first pant leg were like a rough draft, the final, completed version she'd be aiming at from the beginning, a version that she can see and we can't.

• • •

My mother keeps her sweat socks in a white crocheted bag on the handle of the closet door. Her feet never seem to touch the ground, never feel the coarseness of a rug. Even the soles of Hazel's walking shoes must float over sidewalks, streets, fields. It's the look of newness.

"Would you please wash these for me?" she asks on laundry night. "They smell and they're dirty and they... ."

I hold Hazel's white, white sweat socks up to the light and they look and smell brand new. "Are you sure these need washing? They look like they've never been worn."

"I wore them three days ago. Remember when we went for a walk to that park?"

My mother could always see dirt that I couldn't. I imagine the dust settling into her socks, hesitant dust, sliding, shaping around her toes, ankles and heels. Dust is what she's afraid of. Dust is what I'm sure of. I now eat holes in all my socks, like a moth out of control, ever since my parents moved in. My father, with his usual detached brilliance, proclaims: "We're all getting old. We all have holes in our socks." Yes, I am a Moth Son. I have eaten only my own socks, or so I'd like to think. If I look hard enough, I'll probably realize that I've feasted on my mother's socks too. Because I am unable to eat now, I have become the petrified insect on the lip of a clay saucer. Frozen. Bloodless. Before I die, I'll leave my blood on the saucer as a sign of how a son tried to save his parents from themselves. The saucer's lip is bright red, enhances its own complexion. Cracks are showing through. The time to glaze it was yesterday.

The time for a moth to fly was over forty years ago.

Forget I'm here.

Start again.

• • •

What's wrong with Granny now? She knows I'm here but won't talk to me. Last night, I asked her and Grandpa to please turn down the TV so I could study for my exams. No big deal. But they didn't hear me. I had to go downstairs and ask them again to turn down the TV. It looked like they still didn't hear me so I walked quickly over to the TV and turned it down. I told Granny it was me and she nearly chopped my head off with her cane. If it were my sister, Sarah who had to study, Granny would have been so sweet about it all. But it was me, Marie. I don't kiss her butt because of her handicap. I'm sure she can do more. We are not her servants. I know she's not TOTALLY blind. I want to love her but she's not a grandma I can love. I apologize over and over to her but she ignores me, sips from her rye and water, and tells me that's not good enough. I'm crying and crying on the living-room sofa. Granny will not forgive me. PLEASE, GRANNY! PLEASE! My parents are furious, especially my dad. I'm sure he'd throw his mother out the front door, if he could. Mom cuts in, tells Granny to not treat me like that, tells all of us to not give up so soon. Granny threatens to leave anyway, and will not admit she's wrong. My dad gets her suitcase, opens the front door, tells Granny that I'm more important, tells everyone he's going to one of those meetings for some sanity. He's the one who leaves. And Granny makes Grandpa pour her another drink.

• • •

When Hazel first got here, she seemed so helpless and looked like she required constant help. It would be lots of work having her around. Both Mark and I felt we should try anyway. Even though Hazel always says I'm the best woman for her son, she is still a guest here. Period. I was so worried at first and didn't think it would work with Mark and me and our jobs and the girls at school. It seems like we have to serve them all the time, but I'll do whatever I can to help support Hazel. I don't like unnecessary conflict. I feel so uncomfortable in my own house now. Last week, Hazel had another argument with Mark because he tried to protect Marie. Twice Marie had asked Hazel and J.L. to please turn down the television so she could study for exams. Finally, Marie had to run downstairs and lowered the volume herself. Well, Hazel attacked Marie the next day and wouldn't let up, as if Marie had rudely slapped her sightless face. Marie said she was sorry over and over, but Hazel would not accept her apology, to the point where Marie was sobbing. I know Hazel needs care. She must be frustrated, but after seeing and hearing her being so nasty to Marie, I'm forgetting she's handicapped and I'm fighting back like I would do with anyone who attacked my family. "Never ever do that to my daughter again! Understand! If there's a discipline problem with Marie, I'll take care of it, not you," was what I had said. No, I do not support Hazel like I did when she first arrived, and I will not let myself fight with Mark over all this. It's not Mark's fault that Hazel is mean and can't see. He's really trying. We have a duty and can't just throw them out. Even though Hazel says she's legally blind, something tells me she can still see out of the corners of her eyes. I know. I studied her watching TV last week with her head turned sideways and she was commenting on the shape of a scar beneath an actor's eye.

• • •

I have one brown eye and one brown and green eye. I never liked the colors of my eyes. People make fun of me, as if my face were two-coloured. Family often said I looked like Warren Beatty when I was young.

What if I was the one who is nearly blind? I am. I have to be. I sit back and let others shovel the walk. Let someone else take care of Hazel. I've had enough. I've always had too much of her. I say nothing when she complains about her aches, her pains. I laugh, inside, when she pleads, and tell the world she'll be fine. I keep the peace. I pretend to understand that Hazel is having a drink only to help her sleep better. We've tried Detox centers, counselling, and those meetings. One minute she'll say I'm such a fun husband to be with and the next she'll call me a spineless bastard. Why bother anymore! The Don't Drink people say she has to hit bottom and WANT to stop drinking; if not, she'll either go crazy or die. When I think of Hazel, I see a lone fir-tree whose top is wind-bent away from my perfect sky. Gotta keep the family together though. And by saying nothing, I take care of myself.

What about an eye transplant? Hey, I could give Hazel my brown and green eye. She'd never know the difference, even in the mirror. If she did, she'd tell me again and again that I'm only out for myself. Good thing I'm easy-going. Good thing.

• • •

- My mother has always been blind, and so have I; this isn't new. Sometimes, I blame her for making me a drunk too. I never give her credit for any of my twelve years of sobriety. Why should I? We're both sick. We didn't wake up one morning and ask to be ill for the rest of our lives. You can' t get angry at a sick person. I did something about it and she didn't. One of those special meetings is the last house on the block for me.

Something happened between Hazel and me when I was a boy. They say hypnosis can help, but I'm not ready for it. I can't see the difference between my light mother and my dark mother. My brother still wonders about my being my own body of land. My sister says I never stayed on my mother's knee long enough to let her hug me. Sometimes I take friends for prisoners. I cannot totally forgive, but I must or I will go nowhere, again, and insanity will come to stay.

I wear too many sweaters, too many jackets, even on warm days. If I don't get out of myself, I'll be forever trapped behind enemy lines.

A few months ago, before they moved in on me, Hazel said she wanted to die and refused to eat. I sat by her bedside. I fed her tea and Digestive cookies. Her whiskey eyes are still bottle-fed, alive. We should have put each other out of our common misery right then and there, but I wanted her to live. I still have restricted vision.

I was born behind the eyes she used to have.

I was born.

Get over her eyes.

Over.

Them.

• • •

J.L cannot drive anymore and he needs to sell his 1988 Chevy Malibu. I place an ad in the Calgary Herald. The next day, two men named Horace and Clem show up at my front door wishing to purchase the car. Horace is the size of a garbage truck while Clem is short and wiry. Both men are dripping in sweat from walking from the bus stop. They insist on buying the car at our price without even looking under the hood. I've seen tabletops with more brains.

"We'd like to borrow the car for a few days to get a safety inspection done."

"Do you guys have any identification: a driver's license and a major credit card?" I ask.

"Forgot mine at home," says Horace.

"Mine's here in my briefcase here. Oh, shoot...I left everything on my desk at the office but I can give you a receipt," says Clem.

Then, Horace pulls out a pad of blank invoices from a small geology company. When I check the phone book, the company does not exist.

"Brand new company," says Horace.

"Just moved to Calgary," says Clem.

"Sorry. No deal. We need some I.D.," I say.

"Aww, let them have the car for a few days. It's just for a safety check'" J.L. says.

"We better wait, J.L.," Pauline says.

"Look, it's my car."

"Right," says Horace.

"Right," says Clem. "Your car."

"Leave us a number where we can reach you," says J.L.. "I'm sure we can trust you both."

"You have our word. We'll have the car back in three days at the most," says Horace.

"Here are the keys, the registration," says J.L..

"I know honest men when I see them," says Hazel. "Would you two like a drink before you go?"

• • •

When I take my parents to City Hall to obtain senior citizens' bus passes, J.L. says:

"This should be my last bus pass. Imagine, cheap rides on the Light Rail Transit and bus until I die. HA!" I help them fill out forms. Ride 'Til You Die forms.

Hazel clings to my left arm as we prepare to step onto the

escalator. She's afraid of the steel steps. Her cane tap-taps a silent HOLY, HOLY on the moving steel, as if she were asking the elevator for some "slow down mercy". Her lips move in unison with her cane. Hazel's feet belong to two different people and they wait until I tell each of them to step forward. "Now, Mom", I say. Her body sways, staggers, lands firmly on moving steel.

"I don't want to fall or get caught at the bottom."

"You're too fast on your feet. Always have been," I say.

"I don't want to be taken away!"

"From who?"

"From you. You know, like the eye of an asterisk. Somebody has to point which way for me to go. That's you now, right?". And there's my mother, lurching, lurching at the foot of the escalator onto a different step from me, as if she had never lost her sight.

Outside, J.L. says, "We'll take Calgary by storm. Tomorrow, I'll practice going to the mall by using the pass. Three bus-stops and one Light Rail Transit stop." We rest on a busstop bench, and J.L. lights up the second on his three-per-day smokes. He almost eats the tail-end's of his smoke. Inhales a blue-gray sun. In the centre of the penciled sky, I see J.L. riding a cloud with my mother at his arm. They hand out free passes to everyone. Hazel has created escalator passes for those who are afraid. Their destination is unknown and they pretend they couldn't care less.

• • •

Back home, my father turns his back on me, and there is something harsh about it.

"Here's our money for October," he snarls, turning to face me again.

I take his cheque and stuff it into my pocket.

"Aren't you going to look it over, Mark?"

"No. Maybe, you and Mom will have to find your own place. I'll help."

"We'll double what we pay you now!"

"It's not the money, J.L.."

"Just tell me what it is that we're doing wrong and we'll change it."

"It's Mom. She's still playing the same games as when she could see. You know, wanting attention, playing family members off each other, criticizing the girls then telling me how proud she is of them, criticizing you behind your back, reminding each of us not to tell anyone what she said. And the boozing—Mom knows that I haven't been drinking for quite a few years now. Still, she keeps at it, like yesterday, when one minute she was telling the girls to go to hell and an hour later, after a few shots of rye, she gave the girls ten dollars apiece to go spend at the Mac's store.

"Aww, just ignore her. I've been doing it for years. Say nothing."

"There's too much tension in the house, J.L.." Quiet suppers. Sometimes, Pauline and I slip away to our bedroom right after supper and shut the door.

"I just told you to ignore her."

"We can't! We won't anymore!"

"How much more money do you want?"

"I don't want any of your money."

"Sure you do. I've been paying for Hazel and her booze for years now. Why do you think I could only afford my first car at fifty-three. Remember that second-hand, sky-blue Corvair?"

"What?"

"Take the money, Mark. Take the money." My father growls, turning his back on me again.

• • •

Four months after they have moved in with us, I take Hazel for a brief walk into the warm, clean October air and she is like a department store mannequin suddenly come to life. She wears her brown leather boots and long red winter coat, as if at any time a snowstorm might sneak up on her and only her. "I'll be your eyes today", I say. Leaves, nearly all stripped from November trees, crunch in varying octaves beneath our feet. Hazel says, "Know something, those leaves are at different stages of death." We hear the small unpredictable crescendos of the nearby Bow River. Tiny waves. Glassy quiet. I shorten the length of my strides so Hazel can keep up. Green and blue colours filter through the sunlight and bring order to the plumage of a duck's head. Black squirrels scamper by us. Our ankles are a curiosity to the ducks. My mother pushes gently into winter.

"You have no idea what it's like to be blind, Mark," she says.

"You're right. I only know how to see," I say.

"See what?" she says.

"Nothing. Absolutely nothing," I say.

"HA!" she says.

"HA!" I say.

"Why don't you join a C.N.I.B. discussion group?"

"And listen to those bungling idiots feel sorry for themselves!"

She tells me of all the Agatha Christie books she once read late into the night and my father shouting, "Get to bed, Hazel!" But she'd leave his voice in the dark and have another rye and water.

"You and Dad might have to find a place of your own. I wish it was working better but it isn't."

"It's not my fault, Mark!"

Above, the blue Chinook arch reaches down straight through me. I too may get old, lose my vision. My mother and I walk the next while in silence with only her cane click-clacking against trees. Hazel's aging and possible death are probably hastened by too much booze. I've found her bottles hidden in drawers, in sock bags, behind the toilet, in the false ceiling, in her TV, in the clothes hamper and in her pillowcase. Anywhere. Everywhere. Once I even found a bottle in a hat-box. Another time, she replaced her cough syrup with rye and water and left it on the bathroom counter. Nobody knew. I remember when I was a boy helping her out of a taxi and smelling the whiskey in her words. Her arm was a dead weight around my shoulders. I half-held her, lugged her up the walk to our apartment. Inside, her thick, high-heeled shoes dragged against the tin-edged stairs. I helped her off with her coat, guided her into the living-room, and she slumped into a chair, like a bag of potatoes. The next day, Hazel phoned my grandfather and told him about her many imaginary clients she had in her secret hairdressing business: the wife of a C.P.R. vice-president, a famous actress in town for a little Montreal getaway, a talk-show host. The clients were always rich back in the late 1950's and loved to have... just a few drinks.

Today, with no booze, no imagination, we walk. My mother stops strangers, says hello to each, as if her lungs are finally free to create new land-forms in the October air each time she exhales. I hold Hazel in my arms for the first time, and cover her face with the geography of my own kisses. My desperation.

• • •

I know I'm taking a chance but I'll do it anyway. Tonight I'm cooking barley instead of mashed potatoes. I'll throw in some peas and carrots to soften the blow of a sudden change in the weekly menu. What's so scary about barley? We all like it here. It's just a cereal grass with dense bearded spikes of flowers, each made up of three single seeded spikelets and its grain is used in making such items as soups and malt. I should just tell Mark's parents, give them the barley facts. "But, I can't eat something that comes from a tiny beard," J.L. whispers into my ear. "It's not a real beard, J.L.," I say. I watch Hazel shovel down her meat. Poke the barley with her fork. Stab a small mound of carrots. Then Hazel gobbles down a thumbful of barley and peas followed by a quick gulp of water. J.L.'s slow deliberate fork spreads the barley all over his plate, as if the plate were a face-full of beard. He is the last to finish. As I turn my head to get some milk from the fridge, J.L. covers his plate with a paper towel and empties it all into the garbage under the sink. When I look again at J.L.'s plate, there is nothing there but the outlines of faces, each one behind the bars of a cage.

• • •

During supper, after I twist off the cap, the fizzy sounds of ginger ale pour into her glass. Hazel loves her rye and ginger ale. For the first three seconds, she sniffs the bubbles up from her drink, as if the bouquet were more vital than oxygen. She reminds me of a bull sniffing petals off flowers in one of those old Walt Disney cartoons. "Did you know that your sense of smell is the most powerful memory trigger there is?" I try the same inhaling ritual with my glass of pure ginger ale and I'm pulled back to my boyhood.

A friend and I have just stolen as many large bottles of warm Canada Dry Ginger Ale as our arms can carry from one of those green trucks in the huge Canada Dry parking lot. We are chased across an open field, like game, and I'm the only one to get caught. "You should know better," a man in a Canada Dry uniform says. Then I'm led back to the plant where they make Canada Dry and told to sit on a wooden crate by a cooler containing free pop for all Canada Dry employees. "What's your name?" a huge Canada Dry man asks. "Joe... Joe Sanderson," I say as quickly as I can. It's the first fake name I can think of but Joe is a boy I often become when my mother is drinking and abandons me. "Why did you steal our ginger ale?" "Thirsty, Sir. Always so thirsty." "Well here, help yourself. Drink as much as you can. It's cold and it's free. Just don't steal anymore, Joe Sanderson." "Thank you," I say, my mouth rougher than the crate I'm sitting on.

After I told Hazel my Canada Dry story, she lunged into a tidal wave of booze-inspired rage. "I THOUGHT I TAUGHT

YOU TO NEVER STEAL. GO OUT AND BUY A FEW BOTTLES OF CANADA DRY GINGER ALE AND RETURN THEM TO THE COMPANY. BE SURE YOU CONFESS, AND GIVE THEM YOUR REAL NAME THIS TIME. I"LL PHONE CANADA DRY AND CHECK TO SEE YOU'VE DONE WHAT I TOLD YOU TO DO."

And now her head slumps on the table, just as it did that day.

"I'll get her to bed," I tell everyone.

"I'm going to read my baseball book," J.L. says.

• • •

Downstairs in my parents' bedroom, Hazel lies down but is suddenly totally alert. "They're back, Mark. The creatures. Get them out of my bed. There. On the bedspread. On my pillow. Those green glass creatures. Pull the blankets and sheets down. See. Green. Glass. I'm not getting into that bed until you strip everything off it. Right now! I don't care if it was stripped clean, fresh blankets and pillow-cases put on this morning. This is right now! Look! They're back, and it's all your fault, you stole the ginger ale. Strip the bed again. They make me crazy! Take the mattress off. Now. Check under the bed. Do something! Maybe move the bed closer to the window. No. No, better not, your dad tried that once and more slipped in through the cracks. Yeah, the cracks! And what are you going to do about the cracks? Mark! Look at the window, the door. Your father couldn't fix a crack, even if he were falling into one, a big, deep endless one. But you can, yes, you can. You're not like J.L.. You're just like J.L. He never came back. Not like the green glass... ."

• • •

Next day after supper, Hazel feels her way into my den, her cane dragging on the carpet, like a lost musical note from the cassette tape I'm listening to music from the 1940's. In The Mood. Original recordings. Meticulously restored. Digitally remastered. In The Mood. Hazel's music. Hazel asks me to dance with her. Clarinet intro. Hop-to-it music. We improvise. Make quick moves around the wallflower furniture. Feel pity for the empty rocking-chair swaying on its own. Croon better than the clarinets, trumpets or trombones. Smooth. Rich. Clarinets playing off each other like kids trying to out-chant one another. Drummer moving from snare to high-hat with such ease, as if he were calling to his wife in one city and then his mistress in another. Lower. Lower. We're in one of those long ago dance halls where all the women had dance cards and men signed up to ask them to dance. We stop part way. Hazel wraps her arms around me, her nose buried deep in my chest. "You smell just like your father. I just want to love you," she says. And I remember how she loved me when I was a boy, always said I was the man of the house. The song stretches itself almost too far. I gently push my mother away and tell her I'm going to bed, as if she is the girl who asked me to go to a Sadie Hawkins dance many years ago. She's the same girl I refused because her voice sounded like a rabbit chomping on carrots stolen from my garden. But the music gets louder, louder. Clarinets are lovers. No longer children. Luring each other. Up the crest. Stopping. Back down. Up the crest. Stopping. Over. Over the crest. Falling. Falling. Through each other. Drowning. Drowning. Ta-Ta-Ta. Ta-Ta-Ta. Boom!

I climb into bed alone, and immediately feel Hazel wrapping her bare, bare arms around me.

"Promise me you won't die before I do," she says.

• • •

He won't tell me why. Mark seems numb, stiff. Something happened last night with his mother. I get him to sit down, relax and watch the Montreal Canadiens play the Toronto Maple Leafs. Natural rivals. The Habs beat The Leafs again, as if the Toronto players were once again mesmerized by that blue, white and red magic swirling, swirling. Toronto. Toronto The Good. HA! I turn off the TV. Mark hasn't said anything about Hazel and he goes to bed. Hockey. It's not like it was in the old days.

At sixteen, I'm having a game against a team of hearing-impaired players on an outdoor rink. Deaf mutes. Most of the hearing-impaired's wear hockey pads and hockey gloves. Players on my team wear old jackets, woollen mitts and sweaters worn everyday, tweed trousers, longjohns to keep warm. Skating up and down. Up and down. Like knives slicing up the night. Bodies half-crushed into boards, even though no body checking is allowed. My teammates curse at the superior skills of the other team. *Hey, watch that high stick! I'll get you for that elbow! No slashing!* The hearing-impaired players say nothing. Breathe heavily. GRIN. It all happens very slowly at first. One by one their players stare at my crotch. *Must be a bunch of weirdos.* As the First Period winds down, every player from the opposing team gawks at my crotch as they skate by. Some even point at me in the middle of a play, which almost stops the game. *These guys are really strange.* At the end of the first period, I'm sitting on my bench, sucking in that icy air when I feel a numbing sensation in my groin. I look down. See that my zipper is fully-open again. Just about froze my dick off. No wonder those guys were staring. The rest of my team explodes with laughter on the bench and it sounds like hockey sticks slapping the boards one after the other. *Yea, imagine what would have happened if we all had our zippers down, says one teammate. Wouldn't be one hearing-impaired player with his head up! We'd kill them with body checks in open ice, says another. Sure, but imagine the worst! What if our whole team had frozen their dicks off, says a third player. Come on, let's get on with the game. It's freezing out here, another teammate says.* Out on the night ice, every head is up. All zippers are up. Everyone ignores me. Stars blink like a sky scoreboard. Every once in a while, I check my zipper. Sticks are lower. Elbows aren't as high. And no yelling from anyone. The night is filled with bodies bumping bodies, grunts, heavy breathing, creaking skates, slap shots, sticks smacking boards and black, black cold nudging the moon aside.

I tiptoe upstairs to check on Mark, something I never did, when he was a boy. Pauline is asleep, on her side, nearly snoring, her lungs inhaling the dark. I see Mark, naked, eyes fastened to the ceiling, his hands cupped under his head. I hear his sobbing. On the window, raindrops, shine in the dark like transparent insects, ghosts from the rose garden he'll plant next spring. On his groin, Mark's pillow lies puffed, punched, an orphaned cloud.

I never played hockey with my son.

• • •

It happens every night. After supper, J.L. and Hazel are downstairs listening to eight-tracks and records from the 1940's and 50's. Swing Music. Benny Goodman. Count Basie. Tommy Dorsey. Duke Ellington. Guy Lombardo. Perry Como. Mostly though, it's Nat King Cole's voice floating upstairs, like feathers. Every night my father tells my mother that Nat King Cole wasn't allowed to stay at the fancy hotels where he performed, as if Nat were expected to trade in his skin for the night. Used to sleep wherever he could. Then Cole would come back and perform in the same hotel, which wouldn't allow him a room the night before. He played piano only until one day his real talent was discovered. Singing. That voice drifts through me like a cloud going nowhere. "Unforgettable". "Unforgettable." I discover the song for the first time, like the earth feeling its first rain. *Memorable rain.* "Want to go to the Crossroads Flea Market tomorrow, Dad? We'll hunt through the stacks for Nat King Cole eight-tracks. I promise. Tomorrow. I promise," I say, knowing full well J.L. will forget, like Nat King Cole did when he tried to recall those hotels which refused him a room, the same ones he refused to sing in as soon as everyone started wanting him for his voice.

• • •

We're not asleep yet, lying back to back. I hear my mother's white cane tapping into our bedroom. I see her from the corner of my eye, as if she were my only fear. Hazel needs to be inside me to make my darkness darker. The air is so still that I can smell her breath, a bag of rotting bones. Snarling. I hear myself doing it. Snarling. I watch her spin and shuffle out of the room. Her cane click-clacks against the stairs as she heads back down to her room. It doesn't help to tell Hazel that I need time to be alone, my wife and I need privacy. Pauline says, "It's the WAY you let your mother know you want to be alone." Maybe it has something to do with the way I was born or the wolf-way I want to live. Will someone, anyone, teach me how to talk to Hazel before the lone wolf becomes a pack and eats me alive? I hear the tap-tap of a cane, my mother feeling her way down the hall. I hear her mumbling that J.L. and I are selfish because we watched a hockey game together. I don't get up to see if she's made it safely to her room. And Pauline goes to sleep with her back to me.

• • •

I am sixteen years old and it's Friday Night. I'm about to finish mowing the front lawn when my mother comes out with a glass in her hand. "Hey, Mark. It's Friday Night. Only seven o'clock. You should be out having fun with your friends. Here's some money," She sips her rye. "I thought you wanted me to cut the grass," I say. "Well, you heard wrong. Get out of here. Go on out with your friends." I leave. Meet my friends at the pool hall. Play Eight-Ball all night. Win every game. When I come back home at eleven, I hear what sounds like our lawn mower in the backyard. I move quickly to the back of the house and notice the back porch light on and a battery-powered spotlight reaching out into the darkness. The moon is tucked behind a dense cloud. Stars blink as if they will shatter at any moment, blink like worn-out whiskey eyes. There's Hazel gripping the lawn mower with one hand and sipping rye with the other from a plastic tumbler, her own eyes road-mapped in red. When I remind her it's past eleven o'clock and ask her what's she's doing, she snarls: "I asked you earlier this evening to mow the lawn. You didn't even finish the front, let alone start the back. You just took off and left me all alone to do the job. I can't count on you for anything! You're just like... your father!"

• • •

This December morning, Pauline asks me to put up a new calendar because this year is too full, torn, worn out. May as well do it now. The new year begins in three days. I find my hammer and a new tack. See Hazel's face on the head of the tack.

When my mother had rye in her teacup she'd say: "Son, you're the man of the house. Your father has hammer-toes. He's useless. Always dreaming like he was a chunk of cloud or something." And I fully believed her. I hammered in my first thumbtack to hold up a calendar. The head of the tack got shinier and shinier because I kept missing it. Finally, the calendar was hung and the bent shiny tack lasted for the entire year. Putting up curtain rods and shades was hard to do. The tacks kept slipping out once the rod or shade was hung. Never thought of using screws. I'd do it all over again and bash away at the wooden frame. Bashing. Bashing—especially in my parents' bedroom. Man of the house. Hazel would watch me from behind and I'd have to move those damn curtain rods over a little bit here or a little there. Then she'd say, "You just finished a real man's job. Great work! You must be tired. Here, lie down on my bed and we can have a little nap together." Every time I lay down next to my mother, that hammer kept bashing inside my head but I couldn't fix anything. Her warm hands created a new alphabet on my skin. My breathing got shorter. Shorter. I'd want to burrow through the special tunnel I created on these occasions. Feel the cool garden earth all around me. Stop. Dig my fingers into the floor. Leave them there. There. Down. Down. Calendars. Curtain rods. Shades. Crooked. Straight. Everything was crooked, except my hammer.

• • •

So what if my favorite colour is blue! What should it matter to Hazel or anyone else in the family? They're always telling me I should try a new colour. Most of my jackets, coats, suits and sweaters are that dark ink blue. Ink. My colour. Never talks back. I need a new trench coat. Hazel says I wear my clothes until they look like rags on me. We drive to a nearby shopping mall, and we head to the menswear store. Hazel is so hung over that she jokes about shopping for a new head. Sarah holds my arm and smiles with that big grin of hers.

At the menswear store, I say," Just lead me straight to that rack of navy blue trench coats over there."

"Right, Grandpa," Sarah says. Size Forty Tall is what I need.

"Here, try this on," says the salesclerk.

I try on the coat and it fits like a navy blue perfect fit, except for the shoulders, which droop like two uneven parts of the same night sky.

I'll take this one. And I pay cash. I always pay cash. Just stuff my old coat into the bag. I'll wear the new one home.

"Want me to remove the price tags, Grandpa?" Sarah asks.

"No. Let's go!"

In the mall, we stop shoppers to show off my new coat, the price tags showing $89.95, and I invite everyone to touch the fabric.

"Nice coat," says a woman of about twenty.

"Great price," says a middle-aged man whose arms are full of bags.

"Looks sharp," says a young woman wearing what looks like a brand-new wedding band.

"Feels classy," says a man with a child in his arms.

Navy blue is my color. It never talks back to me. Never changes moods. Especially today.

• • •

Always wanted to be a doctor. Always. But we had no money. Squeezed nickels out of dimes. I've told Mark a few times about that dream, and I could tell he never believed me; he'd suddenly study the ceiling or sky, especially when I told him once that I only got as far as Grade Ten in school. Now he's got a Master's Degree and works as a program coordinator for the college and his brother's an accountant. I worked as a traffic clerk for the C.P.R. for twenty-nine years, then a shipping clerk for a cruise line for thirteen years, and finally did part-time work until I was seventy-nine. Used to get free hockey tickets and booze from those moving companies at Christmas when I gave them C.P.R. business or if they wanted me to give them business. I always spread the work around, though, to make sure all the moving companies got a fair deal. Those same companies gave Mark summer jobs so he could attend that precious university of his. I often wanted to remind Mark of this, but he was not easy to get along with, and who needed that temper of his anyway? Never could figure out why Mark was so angry. Anyhow, when I'd come home from a day's work, with the Montreal Star tucked a certain way under my arm, I wished I was dressed better. Mark couldn't believe how fast those suits I bought in Eaton's basement wore thin, especially in the seat. He probably thought I wasn't smart enough to figure out that the cheaper the suit, the faster it wore out. But I knew. Ha! Mark was the kind of kid who had to be told he was smart.

He has always been bright. When I was working for that cruise line, I'd get free trips for Hazel and me down the St. Lawrence River. Mark had no interest in cruises. Said he'd feel cooped up on a boat. Later, Mark thought that it was a good way for me to keep busy when I worked part-time at clerk jobs. The jobs gave me a reason to get out of bed. Felt good, even on those bitter cold winter mornings; it was like the weather was inviting me outside to spend the day with it. I always felt better leaving for work than coming home. I never knew who had exploded at whom when I walked in the front door after a day's work and Hazel would be shussshing everybody up, trying to hide another one of her secrets, like how Mark really hadn't stolen Ginger Ale from Canada Dry. Yes, I loved leaving for work, being invited outside our apartment for the day. Being outside was where I lived. The sky was my family. Still is. Clouds. Grey colours. Blue colours. Sun. Stars. Moon. Black ink of night. Only that heaven of mine knew I could have been a doctor.

• • •

When Mark was seven or eight, I'd sometimes keep him up late on school nights to watch Marx Brothers' films with me: The Coconuts, Monkey Business, A Day At The Races, At The Circus, A Night At The Opera, The Big Store and others I've forgotten. We loved them all. Mark sat on the carpet near my feet wearing his cowboy pajamas with his back to my sofa chair. I remember once telling him that if he laughed any harder, the cowboys would ride off his pajamas. There was Groucho with his cigar and dancing eyebrows. Chico on the piano. Harpo honking his horn, then playing a harp that suddenly appeared from nowhere. All of them either running away from someone or chasing women. I taught Mark how to laugh and he doesn't even know it. No more though. All I see and feel now is his pain. His face looks like it's going to crack any day now. Mark is so closed up, as if he were slowly falling into his own hole in the earth's floor. Hazel and I did the best we could with him. Something's not right.

Once I came home from work early because I had to fly to Cleveland that night for one of my rare business trips and I found Hazel in bed with Mark. Just being motherly, I guess. Mark was about eight. She had both arms around him and her face was all flushed. Hazel told me that Mark had a headache. After that, Mark told me a few times that he didn't like being her "man of the house" but he never said why. I used to just laugh at it all. Hazel was determined that our son would grow up to be a better man than me. "I'll do whatever it takes," she'd often say. Then, there was another time, about a year later, when I turned around at the bus stop and headed straight back home. My cold was so bad I nearly coughed and sneezed my skull off. When I walked into our apartment, I saw Hazel again in bed with Mark. "Mark's not feeling well," she said. And come to think of it, that's when I first realized why I was afraid of Hazel.

• • •

Mark's taken J.L. to hear a Barber Shop Quartet sing those 1940's songs: In the Mood, Moonlight Serenade, Stardust, Little Brown Jug, Tuxedo Junction, Moonlight Bay, Sunrise Serenade, The Little Man Who Wasn't There, My Isle of Golden Dreams, and Pennsylvania 6-5000. I know them all. I could have gone too. I can still hear you know, but it's Fathers' Day. I could tell J.L. wanted to be alone with Mark by the way J.L. muttered under his breath about just going for a walk with his son. I always get left out. J.L. takes care of himself. Same with Mark. Bet they'll come home with a photograph of them both and a picture of that Barber Shop Quartet. Me, myself and I—that's all they are. I bury my face in my hands out here on the deck. I'm staring at the sun through my fingers. I climb its rays and hide somewhere behind the sun. I can see a little bit of light from the corners of my eyes. The wind tightens my face, making me feel like the bottom of a dry ditch. My eyes, nose and mouth are now masked by wind. I wonder if J.L. feels like I do now when he looks up. I want to invent eyesight, invent myself. I pretend to be a mouse hiding among balding flowers. I have so much to share with J.L., lots to ask him, that is, if I can catch him. I feel like a sky mouse chasing J.L. across a cloud as big as a baseball field. I can't see, but I now hear J.L. and Mark calling out to me from an isle of golden sun. They'll have to wait. Unless that gold can be poured into a glass, I want nothing to do with them. Yesterday, J.L. read me a newspaper story about how a famous Big Band leader may have died in a Paris brothel and not in a plane crash as was officially reported earlier. Mark said that the plane, flying from England to Paris, just disappeared. Now they're saying that my favorite musician of all time died of a heart attack in the arms of a prostitute. Oh, how I wish I were that hooker! How I wish!

● ● ●

Mark's taking me out to lunch at the mall. He's probably feeling guilty for the way he yelled at me the other day. He said I wouldn't let him listen to his music alone. I swear he's got a stereo for a heart. When we arrive, Mark slows his walk down to my speed, as if he is obeying my cane code on the mall's cement floor. He's been pushing me away for so, so long. Pushing. Pushing. What I can't say to Mark, I tap in a longer code once I feel that his steps are with mine.

What's in that store window? Tell me what colours you see, Mark. Look carefully at all those shoes, shirts, sweaters and jackets. I'm counting on your good eye, Mark. Tell me especially about the shoes, the skins. You know, leather. Skins. Give me the colours. What might they feel like? Like the hard skin of my hands or the soft skin on the inside of my upper arm? The oily skin on my forehead? Come on Mark, what are you waiting for? Can't you see I'm waiting for your report on the touch, the feel?

54

Food. I smell pizza: tomato sauce, spicy pepperoni, the mild odour of mozzarella cheese. Coffee. Chinese food. Sweet. Steamy. Brown on white. I hate Chinese food! You never know what's in it. Those foreigners, they'll sell anything! Hot dogs. Hamburgers. Buns. Ice Cream. Popcorn. Gawd, I love the smell of popcorn. I prefer food that's easy on my old nose. Get me a ham on white and a 2% milk. You can stick to your hot dog and Pepsi, just like your father. You're so much like J.L. except you're a lot stronger. You can't stand it when J.L. and I fight. And you hide your anger, like frozen juice in the freezer. White bread. It always has to be white. Good. Thanks for cutting my sandwich into more manageable quarters. Helps me feel my way around my food. White bread. I'm not who you think I am, Mark. Yeast made me who I am, made you who you are. Let's pretend we're lying down together for another of our little naps and I'll tell you a make-believe story:

• • •

Once, long ago, I lived in London, England. I thought of joining the ten people a day who jumped onto railway tracks. Instead, I decided to marry a Canadian soldier named Jonathan Louis. Did you ever wonder, Mark, where J.L. really came from? What are you doing, Mark? Bet you're rolling your eyes. Better listen, Mark. Now. My church minister warned me not to do it. Canada had no customs and its frigid winters would turn my bones to ice. But I married J.L. anyway. Better to be in Canada than to continue eating black bread and thinking about railway tracks. The night before our departure, my stomach growled and ached. How much white bread would be served on our boat to Canada? The language of my sleep was slow and jerky, as if I were wading through mud, and my dreams spoke to me in pictures rather than words. Next morning, I was directed onto a ship with other war brides. All the white bread I could eat. There. I stuffed slice after slice into my mouth, stuffing that dark bread down to my toes, like I was trying to bury a secret and swallow the unknown.

I arrived in Halifax and discovered that J.L. had been transferred to Montreal. Still more hours to wait to see my Jonathan Louis. Volunteers from both the Salvation Army and the Red Cross welcomed me and directed me to my Montreal train. White bread bulged from every one of my pockets. Just in case. On the train, I imagined living with my husband in a house with white white walls. I refused to hang anything on the walls. I wanted to see through, through it all. In Montreal, other women studied me, and spoke out of both sides of their mouths, suggesting I had stolen one of their men. I was especially concerned about a long-haired, blonde witch outside church on Sundays who hung around J.L. too long. I was scared. My stomach rose up to my throat. Sometimes, when J.L. was at work, I went for short walks. When I passed people on the street, I checked to see if I was still within hearing distance, and started a delayed conversation with neighbours or friends from home in England. I got better at pretending than at living. Other times, I stayed at home because I was too depressed by the lack of familiar faces from home, and I felt like I was abandoned on a raft in the middle of an ocean. I ate a lot. Started drinking that rough Canadian rye. I listened to the radio, my hand holding up my head, and learned to sing a song about having someone under my skin. One day I had over ten dollars in Canadian coins in my purse, but I was too shy to ask what they were worth or where to spend them. I sent many letters home to England praising my new friends, my new husband, white bread.

In 1951, I did it. I took my first trip back, and I felt like a size seven shoe on a size nine-foot. In Trafalgar Square, English hands were buried so, so deep in English pockets. Nothing like Montrealers whose hands slice up their words with energetic punctuation. I hated England, the British pretense, the hiding. I couldn't wait to get back to Montreal where your dad waited for me with his huge Canadian arms, easy rye, and hockey games on the radio: the Montreal

Canadiens forever. Forever! Not so. We moved back to Halifax in 1953 because J.L. was transferred. And after tha, a transfer back to Monteal again. I remember my bulging pockets: the bread was so white then. The bread was so white. Then. I vowed to never let my pockets become empty. I remember when we first got married. Your father found white bread in all my purses, in every blouse and coat pocket, in my trunk, even under my pillow. My pockets were always whiter than clouds. Bread clouds puffed up with rye.

By 1980, you, your brother and sister were all married, had children of your own. J.L. wanted to leave me for a younger woman, as if I had become a stale piece of bread. The more I tried to please J.L., the more he said that I was way under his skin. He told me to blame it on the war and I wanted to stuff his lungs with all the white bread I could find. Sure, I remember J.L.'s irregular Canadian accent and I hated myself for allowing him and the white bread to lure me away from the dark English bread, but it was done. Yet, he didn't leave me. And I still had my rye. Sometimes, I watch J.L. from behind my blindness, tearing apart a slice of white bread. He usually pats margarine or butter onto the bread and wolfs it down. If the bread is more than a day old, J.L. will make an excuse to not eat any. I have to trick him by sticking older bread into the microwave oven. Old bread. Same trick. New technology. I like to imagine the shapes of white bread muscling down J.L.'s throat and listen to him eat his words.

Mark! Mark! Are you listening? You believe me, don't you? Well, don't you? Look, my purse still contains less money than white bread. Here's twenty bucks. Go back and buy that soft pair of shoes. You know—the ones you told me about. They're as soft as the white bread in my pocket. I hear Mark's words before they leave his mouth, as if he were another one of my "talking books". Something about me paying him to take us both out for lunch. Know something Mark, money could never pay for the way you cut my ham on white into quarters, just like the four corners of our lives. Come on Mark,

can't you hear me? Time to wake up. Quickly! Your father will
be home soon.

• • •

Outside. Fresh air. No boss. Couldn't beat it. I was born to
be a volunteer. On the table in my bedroom is a photograph
of me, in the teeth of a Montreal winter. The picture shows me
resting on a park bench holding an ARRÊT sign in both of my
hands. I wear a red vest with a crest saying: Communanté
Urbaine de Montréal. On my head is a gray tweed cap. My
winter coat and corduroy pants are the colour of rope. In the
photograph's winter day, the green park bench reminds me of
the possible summer of baseball. I cast a straight shadow on
the snow. My eyes squint at the sky, as if the sun were an
enemy. My legs curve over the bench. My back and shoulders
are more erect than the trees in the background. Mark doesn't
know it yet but he's going to have serious back problems if he
doesn't work on that posture of his. He won't ever hear it from
me though; I can't tell him anything without some kind of
blow up happening. Maybe he should get a job as a city volunteer and help school kids cross the street everyday.

As a teenager, I had to sleep on our old sofa for awhile
because we didn't have enough beds. Promised myself I'd
always walk with my shoulders back, my head high just to
keep my back in good shape for the night's sleep. It worked
for awhile until one morning when I bent over to pull my
socks on. My back felt like someone was chopping it in half.
Mark always had his very own bed, so I didn't see why he
fussed about the rats behind his wall or under the floor. So
what? The rats squeaked and clawed at night, but they were
quiet during the day most times. They knew their place. *How
do I get you to straighten up, Mark?*

Once, I was taking the subway home with Mark and I worried aloud about how he slouched in his seat. Then a young
panhandler stopped in front of me: "Got any spare change?"

she asked. "Here's some," I said. When she asked Mark, he slid down even further in his seat, stared out into the tunnel's darkness, and said: "No! Not today." When we reached our stop, Mark and I moved quickly to the exit and right there was a guitar player begging for money. His guitar case was wide-open like a huge black-leathered hand. The open case had only one coin in it, a quarter that looked like a lonely soldier. We listened to him play a song about the blues. I felt the guitar picker's sadness. I threw in three more quarters, three more soldiers. Mark was still moving his lips to the song when he dug deep into his pocket and tossed a single quarter into the case. Usually, I didn't give money to anyone looking for a free ride but the music didn't sound very free to me. I did it for Mark. I wanted to bend over with ease, scoop up every coin. I would send them all back to the mint and have my son's face forged on each and every coin. Then I'd go outside alone and celebrate the tallness of the day, the colour—a blue I wish Mark could see.

• • •

I only know how to raise my eyes and tell Heaven. That's the way I am. Each of my long ago girlfriends rests on her own passing cloud, legs hanging like long, elegant sunbeams. Each girl appears whenever I want her. Nobody sees them but me. Not Hazel. Not Mark. Nobody.

• • •

Jeannette always smells new: fresh perfume, rouge, powder, nail polish, something stiff in her hair. Her clothes are crisp and look like they came straight from a store, not homemade. If she would stand still for a moment, Jeannette could be one of those store mannequins. She often drives over to my place with another couple. Then we all go to the Cinema Paris and later to a cafe for wine. I buy the first round, Jeannette the next. Wine costs ten cents a glass. Jeannette makes more money in one day of modeling than I do in a week as a C.P.R. traffic clerk. She insists that I meet her once a week for lunch and she refuses to hear about my nearly empty wallet. Modeling. That's all she talks about now. All because of that beauty contest she won a few weeks ago. I still can't forgive her for entering that contest. I remember saying: "You'll have everyone staring at you." "Let them stare," Jeannette said. Well, she won the contest all too easily. I know we won't last much longer but I want to try; she makes me forget about my ugly brown and green eye. Before long, I break it off though, mostly because her beauty and brains are too much for me. Too much looking. Too much thinking. Yes, I'd never be able to afford her. She's that sunset pouring more gold into my eyes than I can handle.

• • •

I meet Dorothy on a rainy night at a streetcar stop outside a drugstore. She has the eyes of a cat, even more so in the rain. She is tall, slender, like a willow, and her straight, black hair reminds me of licorice. Dorothy's smile is so wide, it makes me think of two sets of piano keys. What a beauty! One thing leads to another, and I ask her out. The next night, I take her to a Vaudeville show at the Regent theatre. Each of the Marx Brothers tells what it was like being brought up on a turn-of-the-century stage by performing parents. No school. Few rules. Do what Mama says. Really do what Papa says. I buy Dorothy a bag of popcorn. She eats the entire bag herself before the Marx Brothers are half-way finished. "You're a hungry woman'" I say. "Big day," she says. That Saturday, I take Dorothy to the park and she does most of the talking. "I want to sell houses because I'll probably never own one. It's strange but I often dream of marrying a schoolteacher because there's always a regular pay cheque coming in." On the park bench, she does all the talking and I'd rather look up and listen to the blue serene. "I better get you home. Gotta help one of my brothers with something. Then I promised to help my sister." I say. "Don't you want to meet my parents?" she asks. "Weren't those Marx Brothers hilarious," I say. "My parents, don't you want to meet them?" Time to go. Dorothy is fast becoming a monument to herself.

• • •

Vivian seems to be out of love with herself. She is short, heavy and has a face designed for sadness. Every mirror in her house has a picture of a different Hollywood actress. Only a tiny section of the bathroom mirror is left uncovered so she can brush her teeth and comb her honey-colored hair. The rest is filled with Marlene Dietrich's face. Instead of going out on a date tonight, Vivian wants to stay home, cuddle and play cards. "Maybe, we could go out to Woolworth's and split a twenty-five cent ham sandwich," I say. "Sure, J.L.! Sure!" Vivian says. She loves hot, spicy foods. Maybe she's overweight because she is always cooling her mouth and throat with lots and lots of ice cream. I slow down my smooching with her because I hate any spicy food. I can tell. Feels like a foreign country has moved into my mouth. Within two weeks, our kisses have become pecks. Cayenne pepper. Vanilla ice cream. Curry. Chocolate ice cream. Chili. Strawberry ice cream. Tabasco sauce. Pistachio ice cream. A ham sandwich would be out of place. "Think I'll take up playing the violin," she says one night. I don't have time to stick around for her first smile, her first performance.

• • •

I meet Maggie at a Knights of Columbus Dance. She has long orange-red hair, the colour of fire and speaks with an Irish accent. Maggie is slightly shorter than my own six feet, and her breath smells like a newly-opened can of cream corn, my favorite vegetable. We dance the last number. "May I take you home?" I ask. "Why, that's very gallant of you. But, it's pouring rain out there," she says. I have a vague idea of what "gallant" means because I once heard it used in an old film. I can't remember the title because titles are like useless names to me. Gallant! Gallant! The word wants to start a new life inside my head. I dig into my pocket and find my last dollar bill. In the taxi back to her place, I hold Maggie's hand while keeping one eye on her, the rain, and the other on the meter so we don't go past a buck. One dollar. I silently beg. No more. Please! Tick. Tick. Tick. Eighty-five cents. Ninety cents. Tick. Tick. "Right over there," I say, handing the driver the dollar bill. "Keep the change." "Gee thanks, Mister!" the driver says. We slide out of the taxi into the two a.m. downpour. Then up the stairs to her front door. "How about a gallant goodnight kiss?" I ask. We grind our mouths together, and I feel like a movie star with not a cent in his pocket. That's it! "Isn't this rain so romantic?" she says. "Of course", I say. I write down her phone number on the inside flap of my pack of Player's Plain's. And the rain falls even harder after Maggie closes her front door, like the ending of our own movie. My pockets are empty. My twelve-dollar suit from Eaton's bargain basement is drenched. Rain. I try hitching a ride and fail. Catch only the rain. My pants shrink like leaves. I'm left out in the rain.

• • •

It happens fast. I first meet Hazel on a streetcar. Blue-green eyes shimmer, as alive as the crests of ocean waves. Cheeks that bobbed and reddened when she laughed. A voice sounding as smooth as clean sand being poured into a bucket. Straw-coloured hair. Looks like she loves a drink and a good time. It's all done from half-smile to half-smile right there on that streetcar, like one pulley to another on an outdoor clothesline. I know. She knows. After that we get together once a week. When summer arrives, I take a week's holiday by myself away from my traffic clerk job at the C.P.R. Customs work, helping people move, shipping freight. I rent the back parlor from a French Canadian family in Pointe Claire just outside Montreal. Costs me seven bucks. I need the time alone, like I did as a boy wanting time alone in a homemade fort. But this Hazel woman is turning me inside out; my heart is aimed upwards, pushing clouds aside. Every afternoon, I have my one quart of Molson Export Ale, and meet Hazel at the train station. She's already had a few herself; I can tell by her whiskey kisses. She's the one. Hazel laughs at my jokes, especially when I pinch my nose and pretend to sing "Mammy", like that famous singer does. We have a quick supper together saying nothing, saying everything to each other. Then Hazel climbs aboard the eleven o'clock train back to Montreal. In bed that night, I hear her voice, my voice, her voice, my voice, riding through the night like those click-clacking sounds of a nearby train arriving nowhere, arriving everywhere.

• • •

My father pecks at his food, like a giant woodpecker using a blunt beak on a wet tree. "Shut your damn mouth, will ya!' I say. Almost five months. Five months since they moved in with us. At eighty, J.L. is a slow, deliberate eater, as if he were planning to eat his way past his grave. Tonight, his munching is noisier than usual, like those first birds at dawn. J.L.'s mouth holds a dialogue between tongues and gums. I give him more bread with blobs of margarine, and he soaks up gravy, wipes his plate. The smacking sounds in his mouth click out a code of longevity. I listen patiently. *Don't be in such a hurry. Wear the world like loose clothing. Don't be so hard to get along with, he says. Enough. Enough of this warmed-over porridge, I say. What did I do wrong? You're still hard to get along with, aren't you,* he says. As I leave the kitchen, I try to make noises of my own but my mouth is empty, dry. I am fed up with my father. I have discovered who he really is, a new definition of me, me, me. My mind races ahead to that day when J.L. will remove his baseball cap and stand quietly over my coffin. "Why couldn't you slow down, Son? Why couldn't you slow down your anger?' is what he'll say. Then I will sit up in my coffin, tell him he was right and watch everyone, except my father, holding their breaths.

• • •

Families are always proud of their vegetable gardens and they save their fattest tomatoes for absent loved ones. Strangers. Acquaintances. Neighbours. Fantasy lovers. *Here, have a tomato or two. Can't you see that I love you?* My family no longer takes orders; they've outlived innocent games. They keep unconnected items—pencils, pennies, buttons, bolts—in empty jam jars on dusty shelves. The fortunes of my family are told on the skin of a nude gypsy woman leaning against a newly whitewashed wall. The woman is covered in tatoos. Flags. Hearts. Anchors. Lovers' names. Snakes. Lots of snakes. And countries, many countries. The largest country is named after my family, its topography more varied than the aftermath of an earthquake in a coastal city. My city. The city I wish I could leave.

If I could walk away from the bondage of self, I'd inch my way across the world in my parents' shoes, see how they really feel trying to live with me outside iron bars, the cage I built around myself. Then, and only then, would I plant enough tomatoes to feed everyone for ten lifetimes.

• • •

Perhaps this story arrived much too late, but it came when it was ready. I am nine years of age, and I must water the garden that is not ours in the yard below. Stepping out onto the back balcony of our apartment, I convince myself that the garden is the worst-looking in the neighborhood. Overgrown weeds. Yellow. Sparse. Shriveled and squashed tomatoes looking like wounds. Used by rats as a racetrack. The garden is not my duty. We rent. The landlord, who has eleven children of his own, drives a taxi and lives in the ground floor apartment, says to me: "You can be my kid anytime." The landlord is more than pleased to lend me his rusting garden tools. I plant seeds, apply fertilizer. I water, water, water. In a few weeks, the garden is the best looking on the street. At night the rats stand in line for a good feed, then disappear among the garbage cans.

On the front balcony, my father sits on a chrome kitchen chair, pant legs rolled up to his knees and a sleeveless white undershirt displaying maps of sweat. He clutches his one-quart-a-night, Molson's Export Ale. J.L. bends over the railing and says: "Mark, you're way too hard on yourself. Pace yourself. See, I only drink one quart of beer a night. That's enough for me. And remember—we're renting here. Why are you so worried about the front lawn? Ha! I'm surprised you didn't carve your own initials in the back garden." "Aw, come on, Dad. The front lawn needs watering! Can't you see?" "Easy does it, Mark. Easy does it."

After dinner, I leave the vegetable peelings in my kitchen sink. The next time I say "Good Night" to my mother and father, I will force my mouth to shape the love locked in behind these words. Locked in. Set them free. At the moment, I can no longer say anything to my parents. I get up and leave, feeling as if a sudden wind blew in an open window and the window cannot be closed. Outside, vegetables sleep in a brown-faced garden. Soil I know. Soil I trust. Soil nurturing under the comfort of a moon, a moon that knows no seasons. The soil is now barren, overturned to its own night. Buried are those smells of tomatoes, lettuce and carrots. I hear them being inhaled by rats.

· · ·

I hate feeling useless. Mark finally gives me a job. I remove my dark glasses and I can feel my eyes flickering when he leads me upstairs to his bedroom, my cane like an extra foot on the stairs. Mark dumps a basket of clean laundry on the bed and it tumbles, like a waterfall of sorts. All whites. I am asked to sort and fold. I feel for socks, panties, bras; and make separate piles. After I put my dark glasses back on, Pauline and I fall into a rhythm of folding and talking. Words have few creases. Mark leaves to do another load of laundry.

After a long pause lasting as long as ten slow drops from a leaky faucet, I tell Pauline how we took turns doing the laundry when I was growing up. We could not talk as we are now. We were nervous. My mother had mental problems. They gave her shock treatments and all kinds of medicine. Socks were often mismatched and folded unevenly into each other. Underwear was just tossed into a pile. Towels were stuffed anywhere or everywhere. Two weeks before her final Christmas, Mom was bedridden with a severe heart problem, and it kept getting worse. One night, I sat on my mother's bed and sang Christmas carols to her for two straight hours. She was too weak to sing along and just blinked her eyes in sync with my voice. I sang loud and hard, as if trying to organize the music of her death. I remember asking one of my sisters to keep bringing me large glasses of water, lots and lots of glasses. My singing made me that dry.

Then I suddenly sing "Silent Night" for Pauline, sounding like a lone choir member in a cathedral longing for any other voice. I watch her fingers stop folding. Socks, panties, bras— whiter than the white joy behind my eyes. I imagine her fingers leading me in song. My voice is now louder, larger than any religion. Trust me. Trust me. I am a fourteen-year-old singing away my mother's last hours, singing to a God of my own.

• • •

I try harder to make it all go away. A new feeling flashes through my stomach, a feeling belonging to that annoying super-hero who has saved many lives but never his own. My parents have brought with them their Electrolux vacuum cleaner, which is at least as old as I am but not yet ready for a museum. The machine still works but the suction belongs to the lung of a dying man. "It's just like me," J.L. says. "What if I could trade in my old lungs. Even you wouldn't keep up, Mark. Not even Groucho Marx would be able to tell me: "If you can see through a woman, you're missing too much." I say, "You can still chase women around a room with your eyebrows, Dad. Imagine your eyes in an upside-down glass bowl on a table. Three laughing women are there too. Would the women stand a chance, J.L.? Would they?"

I am eight years of age. I pedal an oversized bike around my neighbourhood, trying to sell ice cream bars for The Taste Freeze Ice Cream Company. They've just rented the garage below our apartment for their bikes and ice cream. Forbidden. My parents see it all as child labor. I'd be safer if I hawked ice water from my wagon. The next morning though, I climb aboard an ice cream bike while the real vendors talk profits and selling strategies inside the garage. The sky is lead pencil gray. A light rain hangs like tiny beads from the letters of the Taste Freeze Ice Cream sign painted on each of the dozen or so ice cream bikes parked outside. Rain caught in its own act. Then I look around in all directions, as if searching for a place to hide my conscience, and reach down the cooler's throat. I grab a fistful of bars and run home to watch the Lone Ranger on television. I ride the Electrolux and shout "Hi Ho Silver, Away!" Just me, my horse, Silver, my silver ice cream bars. A hero swallowing his own bullets.

I pull out the old Electrolux and sit on it. My legs are far too long and drape over the sides, like two lost pieces of rope. I try to remember the hero feeling I had when I agreed to have my parents come live here. I ride across a dry prairie, knees dragging through the dust.

• • •

I decorate the Christmas tree with my sister, Sarah, while Granny and Grandpa watch TV at the other end of the room. One by one, we fill the branches with ornaments that don't shine. My father just had another argument with his parents, something about Grandpa being capable of helping Granny more. Dad always has a hard time getting into the Christmas spirit but it's worse this year. I sing "Silent Night" with Sarah. I hear my father forcing a hum from deep inside his chest. He approaches us at the tree. It's the closest I've seen him get to a Christmas tree in years. In his hand is an old photograph of Sarah and me on Santa's knee. My father can't recall who took the picture. Then I remember him telling me about the huge glass and paint manufacturer that piled broken shards near the railroad tracks behind his apartment house. Whenever the Christmas balls on his tree did not glisten enough, he would go to those piles of glass and climb to the top of the tallest pile. There, he'd shut his eyes because of the blinding sun reflecting off the glass. After, he brushed aside the snow, found the largest piece and cleaned it off with his sleeve. Imagining it was a Christmas ball, my father picked it up and pretended to hang it from the sky. Then he'd pick up a second piece, brush it off and hang it next to the first shard. Soon, dozens of shiny pieces glistened from the sky all around him. The sun was his angel and the Christmas tree was his life under glass. He told me not long ago that his own mother usually drank more at Christmas. Lots more. She'd forget to turn on the oven for the turkey. Fall into the Christmas tree. Vomit on the gifts. One second she'd say mean things about Grandpa, like how weak-spined he was, and in the next moment she'd say how special his sense of humour was. Every Christmas Day my dad would run outside to his glass pile and hang more glass pieces from the sky. It's the only Christmas tree my father ever believed in. And that's why Sarah and I always did the decorating with my mother. Now it's just Sarah and I who do it. I know this story well because my dad repeats it every year as soon as November begins, as if he were re-creating his own Remembrance Day. I wish he would forget. I wish he would remember: Us.

• • •

There's J.L. hunched at the front door, his fingers fumbling, grasping and eventually joining the zipper on his navy blue winter coat, the zipper of his two halves. He zips it up, zips it down, like the short bursts of a harpsichord. There's my father conducting an orchestra from one of his Big Band records, dressed in a white dinner jacket and seamless smile. The smooth gliding of his baton taps in rigid confusion. J.L.'s fingers belong to many different people. He practices doing his zipper twice more, then lights a cigarette. Smoking inside makes us all sick so he must do it outside where clouds in his sky couldn't care less. Then J.L. grabs a lawn chair and heads out into the December air. He unfolds the lawn chair just outside the front door, and clumps down like a boulder in a giant sling. It begins to snow. How beautifully incongruent he is, in the lawn chair with his navy blue winter coat and gray tweed cap! The snow now falls more heavily. He brushes the flakes away from his face, but his head and body are soon covered in white, his hand a shelter to his half-smoked cigarette. The smoke, his breath, cold air, blowing snow, a wish trying to come true. I become more gentle, more submissive; irritants leave me. I am smoking and drinking again. I get along with everyone and can now work my way into any conversation. J.L. was always a light smoker and drinker. He didn't burn holes in clothes, furniture. Never scared me with his carelessness. My father is now persistent, diligent with Hazel, as if she were a robin feasting on old berries in the backyard. When a substantial number of berries have been consumed, the robin staggers across the grass, its voice broken, its beak unsure of its aim. Then the bird falls to its knees in the wet, wet grass and half-digested berries spurt from its throat. J.L. remains hunched in his lawn chair, collar turned up. He pulls his cap lower, over his eyes.

• • •

I LOVE LUCY means we all love Lucy and tonight, we all settle down to watch videos from my black and white boyhood. The signature song. The swollen heart. I LOVE LUCY. I LOVE LUCY. Lucy dresses up as Harpo Marx to surprise the children at her son's birthday party. Lucy's husband, Ricky, decides to have the real Harpo show up but doesn't tell Lucy. The real Harpo meets the Lucy Harpo face to face; and both pretend they are standing in front of a floor-length mirror. Open mouthed. Close mouthed. Big eyed. Squinting. Small steps. Big steps. Moving backward. Forward. Ducking. Bobbing. Weaving. Hands moving in tiny circles. Big circles. Bigger circles. Fingers pointing upward. Downward. Arms folded. Unfolded. Faces grinning. Frowning. Grieving. Pouting. Mirror, mirror on the wall, who's the best Harpo of us all? Each move timed perfectly until the neighbours, Fred and Ethel, burst into the room singing HAPPY BIRTHDAY. My father sees. I see. Even Hazel must see from the music of the words. The dialogue, the TV laughter, our laughter, make my mother laugh and cry from the other side of her blindness. I feel so young now, wearing short pants on a Montreal street. Maybe too young. I study J.L.'s face so he can once again teach me that laughter comes from an open soul. There's J.L.'s face, lines moving up and down, folding, faulting, like landforms from another planet, or in a silver mine. His eyes water, roll. His mouth half-open. J.L. glances at Hazel, at me, as if he were making sure we understand. He's now on his feet and pretends to pull rubber chickens from under his sports jacket.

I stand. Do the same. Pretend the jacket. Pretend to not be me. "Mark, your laugh sounds exactly like your father's," my mother says, wiping away the tears from her eyes. Hazel's voice is lighter, richer. She is young, full of promise, like a wailing saxophone at a Hollywood, ocean front party. And the real Harpo chases my mother across the sand, honking, honking that bicycle horn of his.

• • •

On a morning that is unleashing the sun through my window, I awake to the sounds of father teasing and mother giggles echoing from the air vent near my bed. It's my father doing all those old and new voices again: W.C. Fields, Jack Benny, Red Skelton, Jonathan Winters, Robin Williams and even André Philippe Gagnon singing like Mick Jagger. Their laughter increases until the vent nearly shakes itself free into the light. I tiptoe downstairs. "Mind if I come in?" I ask.

"No, come on in, Son," J.L. says.

"Sure, come on in," Hazel says between bursts of laughter.

"You been in the sauce again, Hazel? I ask.

"No."

Both my mother and father are in the same bed under blankets, like motel lovers, for the first time, I guess, since J.L.'s prostate removal. I forget that I am so tired of the fact that they are always there coming between Pauline and me and not even know they're doing it. No time to be alone with Pauline. No time to tell Pauline that I'm worried about how she holds her feelings down since my parents moved in. Hazel's laughter slowly pours itself, like sugared water, into the corners of their bedroom. She paws at J.L., like a bear cub. "Cut that out, Johnny. I'll pee in my pajamas," my mother says.

Nobody would guess that this man and woman now sleep in separate beds. A knot starts to form in my stomach. I am afraid that I won't have this love in my own old age. Then J.L. makes more funny faces and voices. The gut knot disappears, reappears. My mother loves J.L., his comic faces, his easy sadness, that honest awkwardness of his bones. The audience is his, all his.

• • •

Shopping is done without a list. First I have some groceries to buy, and J.L. wants to come into the store with me. "You might need some help," he says. Hazel stays in the car. When we enter the store, J.L. heads straight to the Baked Goods Department. As I'm bagging a few tomatoes, he ambles towards me with a lemon meringue pie the size of a small moon in his hands, and he reminds me of a high school baseball player carrying a winning trophy home to his mother. "Bought this for you and Mark," he says. Mark and I and the girls never eat lemon meringue pie. "We both know who you bought that pie for, right?" Then J.L. drops his head, shrugs and shuffles his feet. No big deal! I carefully place J.L.'s pie on top of the cabbage, lettuce and spinach inside the basket. Finishing my grocery list means I have to keep shifting J.L.'s pie so it doesn't get crushed. It's as if I am J.L.'s mother, protector of my boy's trophy. After the check-out, J.L. carries the plastic bag containing only his pie to the car. "I'll drop you both off at Eaton's and come back in half an hour," I say.

When I pick them up a half-hour later, J.L. nearly flings Hazel into the back seat of the car like a rag doll. I won't tell Mark. He's not sleeping very well these days. He says, *Why the hell should I suddenly have to take care of her now when she didn't take care of me all those years!* When I look outside my window, pretending not to notice, two robins collide in mid-air. "Come on, get your bony ass into the car. NOW! And don't trip me with that damn cane!" "Easy, J.L.", I say. "She's your wife." Hazel looks like a scarecrow, weaving and bobbing in the afternoon wind with a huge Eaton's chocolate bar under her arm. J.L. shoves her over in the back seat. "Come on, move it," J.L. growls. Hazel taps me on the shoulder with the chocolate bar, and sings: "For you, Pauline. Just for you and Mark and the girls. "Then Hazel turns to J.L. and shouts: "FOR GOD'S SAKE, J.L.. FOR GOD'S SAKE!"

Then J.L. says, "WAIT, Pauline. I need to pick up a couple of shirts. You stay in the car, Hazel," sounding as if Hazel wouldn't know the difference between a man's shirt and pantyhose. I take J.L. back into Eaton's to Men's Clothing. He buys two shirts, one pink and one blue, with button-down collars. He is happy. In his own kind of heaven. The skin on his hands is as thin as tissue paper, and he holds the bagged shirts to his chest like two oxygen tanks. When we return to the car, he says, "Look at my new shirts." But Hazel's face is mapped with tears.

We still shop for a new dress for Hazel for their fiftieth wedding anniversary.

"You want to look your best," I say. "Mark and I are throwing a little party for you and J.L.."

"You and Mark have been so kind. Must be tough having us living with you," Hazel says.

"Yea, must be hard some days," says J.L..

I drive them over to Woodward's, and this time J.L. stays in the car to read one of his baseball books. I take Hazel inside, and I watch her touch racks and racks of dresses. I describe each dress in more detail now, but Hazel says they are too bright, too young, or too long. My own eyes surprise me again and again: "Here's one Hazel. It has middle green leaves on a white, white sky. Here's another one with yellow and blue stripes that look like two highways. This dress has such a soft pink colour, it could put you to sleep, Hazel."

We find the second dress Hazel tried, and she wants it. Modeling her new purchase, Hazel parades around the store without her white cane. With each compliment I give her, Hazel skips a step or two.

"You'll need your cane to fight off all the men at your party," I say.

Finally, we are done, me with my Eaton's chocolate bar, J.L.

with his lemon meringue pie and shirts, and Hazel with her new dress. At home, she tries on her new elegance and prances around the sunlit rumpus room. I dance with her. She is new. Her price-tagged arms create shadows, that carve up the walls.

J.L. pulls the shirts out of the bag, unwraps both right then and there. Hazel is still twirling in her new dress but congratulates him on his great taste. Then he realizes. Wrong neck size. He tears the cellophane, the bag. Flings everything all over the room. His arms flail like a couple of broken weather vanes. His feet stomp, though he's sitting down. His face is as red as the erratic glow of a morning sky. Then J.L. is on his feet, teeth grinding, snarling, ranting: "It's your fault, Hazel! You didn't measure me! You didn't measure me!"

• • •

That evening, my mother is sitting on the toilet seat lid, her knuckles whiter than the lid itself. Sarah is cleaning out a cut on Hazel's knee with alcohol. "AAAAAH, that burns!" Hazel shouts.

At the bathroom door, my father leans against the doorway with a Marx Brothers' biography at his chest. I notice a tear in his pants at the knee.

"What happened, Dad?" I ask.

"We both slipped outside Eaton's at the mall when we went back a second time. Nothing serious."

"Are you sure?"

"Your mother's knee is fine. You know your mother," he whispers into my ear. "She just wants attention. I scraped my knee too but I'm fine. We took a taxi home."

And now Hazel limps towards me at the doorway.

"Want me to double-check your knee, Mom?" I ask.

"That's very thoughtful of you, Son," she says.

Then I do a quick pull-off of her bandage.

"Just a minor cut, Hazel," I say.

"Her whole life is a minor cut," J.L. again whispers into my ear.

"You won't need stitches, that's for sure. You were probably more scared than hurt, Mom," I say.

"How the hell can you tell, Mark?"

"O.K., sit back down. Let me have another look."

"Why bother, Mark?" J.L. whispers.

"I heard that, J.L.! All you really care about is yourself and your lemon meringue pies."

"Yea, sure," my father says, still at the doorway and now browsing through his Marx Brothers' book. "Listen to what Chico says: "I always chased women for one thing and one thing only and the women knew exactly what I was doing even when they acted like they didn't? I did as much performing off the stage as I did on it. And these women never stopped acting."

"Forget those guys, J.L.! My knee needs another look," Hazel says from the toilet seat, her arms and legs protruding at angles to the toilet bowl.

So I try. I really try. I imagine Hazel in her school uniform. On the girl's knee is a fresh bandage covering perfect skin that has been scraped raw. She asks if she can wear the bandage as a badge.

"Imagine. Imagine getting paid for all that acting," my father says.

• • •

Although I believe that Mark is doing this out of sheer duty only, we invite friends over to celebrate J.L's and Hazel's December, fiftieth wedding anniversary. I often wonder if Mark ever loved his parents. His is a TV love, a sitcom love. Anyhow, Sarah and Marie have painted Hazel's nails, done her makeup, and she was at the hairdresser all afternoon getting a perm and a manicure; I can smell the tart nail-polish and that combination of rotting eggs and chemicals on her head. Hazel wears her new, blue dress with a waterfall of navy blue beads cascading down the front, and a pink carnation, shaped like a flattened nose for a corsage. She smells like a cosmetic factory. Her half-crooked face tries so hard to force a smile that some of her makeup is peeling off from the tops of her cheeks. In his grey suit, J.L. could easily be a doorman at a once prestigious hotel clinging to a piece of its past; his eyes blink and sparkle, like the only two lights in a tall, straight Christmas tree; his sweet-smelling after-shave lotion is causing his shirt collar to glue itself to his neck, but he says," Bring on the night."

Guests arrive and gifts are given. Many presents are from strangers. Our guests are unusually quiet, as if they aren't sure why they are here tonight. J.L. acts like he's known everyone for years: "Come on in. Let me take your coat. Good to have you here tonight. Is that a new suit you're wearing? Great to see you! Have you lost a few pounds? Wow, you look ten years younger tonight! Still working too hard? Love that tie you're wearing. Tell us one of your great jokes tonight. Let me play a song you like. Bet you could sing with any Big Band. What would you like to drink?" Mark's father has words for everyone, and works the room, as if he were inviting the world to stand with him under admiring stars.

After each present is opened, J.L. warms up the crowd, charms his way around the room. "Once I tried to paint our bathroom with blue enamel. The colour was so dark and the smell so awful that the family stopped teasing me about the smell I usually left there. What a mess! The paint was as thick as tar and I had to do the entire job all over again after everything dried. Actually, I had to redo the job twice. Never painted again after that. And the bathroom, well, I bet you can still smell nothing but that enamel thirty-five years later." It's that same story again, the one Mark's father always tells to poke fun at himself. He never acknowledges Hazel, over by a wall quietly retreating into her blindness, as if he and only he knew that her memory is dimming. Tonight there is a second story.

"One time, I was driving home and the rain fell so hard, I couldn't see a thing and had to pull over. I sat there, windows rolled up, sweating through my fear. I couldn't move, even after the rain was gone. A policeman stopped and asked if I needed help. I was frozen there, motor humming, and my knuckles whiter than a rain cloud. Then I asked the cop if it had stopped raining yet. Funny, eh?"

Against the wall, Hazel is lost in her own darkness, but still manages to half-smile at bits of J.L.'s stories; she continues to allow him the spotlight she cannot see.

"Then there was the time when I fell and ripped my trousers at a dance. I had this beautiful girl in my arms and tried to show off. Well, I just slipped and slammed to the floor on my butt. Ripped my pants at the crotch and... "

By the wall, Mark's mother has disappeared; in her chair another woman yells: "I'm also part of this fifty year journey!' Then she waves her fingernails, like tiny, flashing, red knives.

• • •

My mother has done it again. "My stomach's sick. I've been retching like crazy. Must be something I ate," she says. I take her back and forth to the toilet bowl. Place cool cloths on her face. Spoon strawberry extract into her mouth. Crush Milk of Magnesia tablets into water. Nothing stops the nausea. We take my mother to an emergency ward where she undergoes tests. I find myself stroking Hazel's forehead, even kissing it gently two or three times, as if I were suddenly able to heal her. I smell whiskey on her breath. Hazel was weaned on rye. She was sneaking drinks at her anniversary party. Hazel is a sick, helpless child, like the girl who cried wolf. J.L. shows no feelings, sighs, exhales loudly in a chair beside her bed. "She'll live," J.L. says. After three hours, the doctor says," We've found nothing wrong with her. Might be a bad case of indigestion. And try to keep her away from the liquor. She can rest here awhile before leaving." J.L. yawns and then disappears to go buy a Coke. Then we wheel Hazel out to the car. On the ride home, my father says, "I knew it wasn't serious. You'll be fine."

"ALL YOU THINK ABOUT IS YOURSELF!" Hazel yells.

At the age of six, I'm kneeling by the toilet bowl with my stomach jumping for the ceiling. Hazel, in her pajamas, enters the bathroom. "Boy, are you ever sick. Peeeyouuu!" "My stomach keeps working on its own, Mom," I say. When I turn towards my mother, her left hand holds her pajama top to her nose as her right hand presses a cold face cloth on her forehead. There, aimed straight at my face, is her naked breast. The nipple is alert and the colour of soil – a large, supple cone of flesh. I turn my head. Pretend to ignore the putrid blasts of rye on her breath.

• • •

Back home, my father carves each of my mother's tablets on the kitchen table. Pill by pill, J.L. slices and drops the two halves into one of many pill bottles. Two halves of my father: one craves complete solitude, the second, a crowd. J.L. insists on being left alone in the kitchen.

Now, he makes his famous fudge which he calls "Maple Cream". Brown sugar, whipping cream and melted butter. He stirs together on the kitchen stove with a gentleness that could melt rock candy in seconds, and his mouth is open half-way. He won't let the stove get too hot. The smell drifts through the house, and we wait with the taste buds of giants. When it's ready, J.L. spoons the mixture into two glass pie plates and orders everyone to stay out of the kitchen. After the fudge has cooled off on the kitchen counter, my father carefully slices it into chunks, and fills two bowls. One bowl goes into the fridge and is saved for everyone in the family. The second disappears into his bedroom where he hides it behind a Saint Anthony statue. When everyone is asleep, except for Saint Anthony, J.L. gobbles down the entire bowl there in the darkness, as if he were only following the dictates from Hazel's holy stars in his bedroom.

Now, after each pill is halved, I want to split them into quarters, into eighths, into sixteenths. I slip another pill into Hazel's hand and give her a glass of water. She coughs a new cough. "How about a couple of teaspoons of syrup to take the edge off your cough?" I ask. Hazel nods and I spoon some into her mouth. "Thank you so so much, Mark!" Gratitude from my mother drifts between the rhythms of her white cane tapping on the stairs and I prepare for a lone walk. I tie a black scarf around my head, pretend that I am blind and stumble around the hallway, banging into walls and closets. Suddenly, I hear Hazel moving towards me. Closer. Closer. Our fingertips brush. We bump into each other. My mother wraps her hands around my head, her hands, like new leaves on a plant that lives only in water. "Dress warm", she says. "Dress warm."

When I return home from my walk, she has ran away. No one has noticed. On the kitchen table, an open bottle of whiskey is missing more than half its label.

● ● ●

I wish Mark and the rest of the people in his house would just disappear. It's just me and my whiskey and I feel like a painting on a wall. I touch my toes; they want to run away. Blood swells in my hands. Need another shot of rye. The house is on fire. The fire leaps in my belly. I drink to quench it more and more and take away the pain. I'm falling from a smoldering paradise, down to a hell of icebergs. My face slips through my neck, hides inside my stomach and prepares for the heat to come. The whiskey sliding down my throat has a life of its own. I drink because I have to. I drink because I hate myself. I drink because I don't fit in anywhere. Never have. When I was a girl my father took me to a Girl Guide meeting hoping I'd want to join; I lasted ten minutes and begged my father to take me home because I quickly realized how much I hated uniforms, clubs, and everyone doing the same thing. I don't feel anything now. Fear. Gone. Last night I was so drunk, only Mark's dog, Golden greeted me near the bathroom door. Everyone else had shut me out behind bedroom doors. I appreciated Golden's company and gave him a saucer of whiskey and table cream. Golden lapped it all up and had great difficulty going up or down the stairs. Tonight, I offer Golden another saucer of whiskey and table cream but no matter what I do, the dog refuses to drink. Maybe, I should push his face into the saucer. Stupid dog bit me! Bastard! Probably thinks he's saner than me. Ha! But the fire, the fire. I'm on the last step forever with the fire waiting, and the ice in my hand. Get me fire!

Get me! Hurry. Help me find another father for my children. That J.L. only thinks about himself. Always has. I stand in the dark in my loose robe; I move up and down, getting ready for another blackout; my body multiplying and metamorphosing into a water storage tank the size of a house. Now, I'm being towed up and down a gentle, sloping highway, my highway. I move past houses that are questions: Who was that woman who kept phoning J.L. for a few months? What have I done to hurt Mark? All I did was have a nap with him once in awhile. Why couldn't Mark be the man of the house? Right now I am fit, ready to answer for myself. I salute my new blood with another raised shot of rye, blood that tastes like vinegar, blood moving like paragraphs through my veins. I smell something burning. If Mark and the others won't leave, I will. I leave. I am running away.

• • •

I'm outta this place. Now. No more! Bushes. Walk slowly. I know the route to the park bench where I went with J.L. a few times. The air feels so easy, so warm on my face. Fresh smells. People must be digging up their gardens. Stupid curb! Use my

cane. Use my cane. If I make it to that bench, I can sit and figure out what to do next. I love my rye. Mark stopped drinking a few years ago and I hate the way he talks about those
special meetings of his and spouts that special prayer. I've had
enough of him and everyone else. I should have left long ago.

No one cares about me. Oh, stop honking you jerk! I'll get
off the street in a moment. Can't you see I'm blind! No, I don't
need your help. Just point me to the small park around the
corner. Yes, I can do it on my own. Just point me. Wonder
how I look stabbing my cane everywhere in the middle of the
street. Everyone thinks my brain doesn't work too. Idiots! I
know a few places where I could shove this cane. That'll make
'em listen. The avenue traffic is getting closer. I must be near
the corner. Turn right. Turn right. Not far now. Oops, sorry.
Banged into what feels like a baby carriage. That kid has a
good strong cry, just like Mark's. Sorry. Sorry. Could you tell
me how far the little park is? What? Just hold on to the edge
of your son's baby carriage? Well, that's very thoughtful of you.
Think I will. I feel the carriage's wheels bump over the sidewalk and I use my cane to watch for branches, bushes and
telephone poles on my right. Suddenly I feel the carriage dip.
Must be the alley. Those stones scare me. Could lose my bal-
ance. Almost there. We're here. Great! Could you please guide
me to the bench? Just over to the right, I think. Yes, it's safe
for me to be out here on my own. I'll be all right. Thank you.
Thank you. Ahh! I'll rest for awhile. Figure out what to do
next. Only the sun listens to me now. Wish I could understand
the sun and wind like J.L. does or why gardens do what they
do like Mark does. That sprinkler across the street speaks my
language. I need a shot of rye. What's that song? Dah, Dee,
Dah, Dee, Dah, Dee, Dee, Dee, Dee—Dah, Dee, Dah, Dee,
Dah, Deeee—Dah, Dee, Dah, Dee, Dah, Dee, Dee, Dee,Dee
– sounds like a kid's song. It's that ice cream man on his electric cart. I wave my cane like a magic wand and yell out. The
song stops. Yes, I'll have the most expensive ice cream treat
you have. Give me the best. Thank you. Thank you. Oh! Oh!

I didn't bring my purse. What do you mean you want it back! I've already had a lick and a bite. Okay. Okay. You'll get your money. Can you drive me to the liquor store first? It's only a few blocks away. You will? Oh, thank you so much. You've seen me around the neighborhood? Then you know you can trust me. Right? You do? Good. The liquor store is that way. Climb on? Sure. Sure. Give me a hand will you. Do I like going for a ride? Watch me. Watch me. Listen, I can sing your song.

• • •

Where is she? I've looked all over the house. Backyard. Frontyard. Hazel could never make it out there on her own. I run out to the front of my house and hear the ice-cream vendor's singsong. That's all I hear. Then I hear my mother's voice singing the birds to attention. I run up the street, turn the corner and see Hazel perched on top of the ice cream cart and her cane weaving, as if she's a conductor, into the sunlight. MOM! MOM! Where are you going on that ice cream cart? GET BACK HERE! HEY, STOP THAT CART! I run. And run. MOM! MOM! WHERE ARE YOU GOING WITH THAT ICE CREAM GUY? I run harder but I can barely keep up. MOM! MOM! I know she hears me. So does the ice cream man. "Faster, faster. It's just around the next corner," I hear her say. STOP! STOP NOW! That does it. The cart stops in the middle of the road. "Where do you think you're going, Mom?" I ask. "Home to you, Mark. I owe this man for my ice cream and a bottle. Would you mind paying him now? I'll repay you at home. That's a good boy. I can always trust you." "But weren't you coming back to the house?" I say. "Maybe I DID know where was going then, didn't I?" she says. I help her down off the cart and pay for her treats. "Get your hands off me!" Hazel says suddenly. "I'm going with the ice cream man." And Hazel jumps back on the cart, her cane clicking and clacking against the steel sides. "Will you please do something about your mother?" the ice cream vendor finally says. "She has her bottle and her ice cream and I've got to finish my route." "Mom, let's just go home. Please." "I need a rye and water", she says. "Right, Hazel. Right," I say.

"Don't we go left, Mark? Don't we?" she asks. "Lordy, I need a drink", she says, her voice as dry as a drained creek.

• • •

When we arrive home, Hazel acts like she never ran away, but remembers to pay me for her booze and ice cream treat. "I'd better rest for awhile. Think you could forget about yourself for a few minutes and get me some tea and Digestive Cookies?" she asks. "Don't start with that again," I say. "Here, sit at the kitchen table and I'll get you your tea and cookies. Why don't you tell me about the times you went skiing at sixteen down Mount Royal in Montreal?" I say, hoping to change the subject of everyone in the entire world being self-centered except Hazel. And she starts. My mother forgets she's seventy-eight, nearly sightless, bitter. Hazel is pretending to be so fashionably dressed on Mount Royal, as if she were trying to insult her entire working-class neighbourhood. Her descents are Mount Everest-like. Her long, thick, brown, curly hair swoops everywhere behind her, creating the alphabet of her absolute joy. I read the words her hair makes. I AM GOOD. I CAN DO IT. THEY'RE ALL WATCHING ME. Hazel sips her tea between words and her motions become smoother and smoother. I imagine a light snowfall and my mother thrusting through it, holding her breath, the puffing cadence of her laugh rolling, rolling to the bottom of the hill where she stops, puzzled, because nobody bothered to wait for her.

• • •

I can't believe Hazel just left me like that, taking off on an ice cream cart and Mark having to run after her. She said, "I only came back because I forgot my purse." The only other times I've seen her take off like that were when we went swimming sometimes; Hazel could spend her life in liquids. I slid my red chair over to the window and looked and waited. It all happened while I was watching the Montreal Canadiens beat the Calgary Flames. She questioned my game. Again. Her note said she was leaving me to become Agatha Christie. Hazel's listened to every Agatha Christie book tape. Agatha was important. Agatha solved mysteries. Agatha knew all about murder. Agatha knew. Also, her note mentioned that I wasn't old enough for her right now. Crazy. How can a man suddenly become too young for his wife? While I waited near the window for Hazel to be brought home, I thought of our old Montreal apartment where the kids spent most of their youth. I am sitting by the living-room window in the old place waiting for one of the kids to come home, which is not normal for me because Hazel usually does that. The hockey game is on, with a black and white version of the Montreal Canadiens winning their fifth straight Stanley Cup in the spring of 1960, with a record-tying eight consecutive playoff victories. Under the window, the valved arm of an old radiator twists up from the floor like a steel snake. A second arm sticks out from the top of the radiator and it too is crooked. The radiator screeches and gasps. Wish I could have stayed in 1960; I knew exactly where radiators stood and I still believed Hazel most times. Not one living thing by the window needs warming, except my shadow. Ha! Hazel would never leave me for an ice cream man! She needs me. She needs me.

• • •

It is neither day nor night. A man climbs into his car, shotgun tucked under his arm. He lays the gun on the front seat next to his camera. "I'm going to kill her!" he shouts.

The woman drives away, the car weaving down the road, but he's determined to get her. A few blocks later, he chases her down. Colour drains from her face when she looks in her rear-view mirror. As the man emerges from his car to complete the job, he inadvertently grabs the camera instead of the gun, and dashes towards the woman's vehicle. She nervously rolls down her window. "For once you're going to listen to me. You don't know how lucky you are, how close you came to dying." Then he points the camera at her, snaps the shutter and strides back to his car, the camera hanging like the head of a dead panther after a nighttime kill. Finally, the man sees himself in his mother, feels her pain, tastes her booze going down his throat, her insanity. What happened to her is now happening to him. He's doing the same things over and over again, like saying he'll only have one beer but drinking twenty. The man is powerless, and blames his mother, as if she were the one who cast that booze spell over him.

The man is a boy again and his mother takes him along to buy the groceries on a Friday after school. She buys one six-pack of beer and tells him it's for the weekend. At home, the six-pack is slid onto the coffee table in front of her. The boy goes out to play. Right away, the mother calls Dial-A-Bottle for a twenty-six of rye and another six-pack. She slides the rye behind the sofa and places the second six-pack in the veg-etable tray in the fridge. She knows her son or husband would never look there. Then she downs two quick ones from the vegetable tray stash and another one from the coffee-table, followed by a few stiff gulps of rye. Later, when the boy returns, he cannot understand how his mother got so drunk, so fast, on so little.

The man slides into his car, waits, tugs the picture from his camera. I tap on the man's window and he hands me a pho-tograph. There's my mother's shot: her horrified but finally silenced, white, white face.

• • •

Hazel is lost again.

Where did that wife of mine go? I've searched everywhere

around the house. Bet she took off. Hope she hasn't run away with the ice-cream man again. That Hazel drives me nuts. Truth is I'd like to take care of her more but I don't know how and I'm afraid to ask anyone in case I do my usual lousy job. I'll look outside. It's cool, wet. Roads and sidewalks look slippery. Maybe she's at that little park around the corner. I'll go check. She's probably sitting on that bench waving her cane at the birds and squirrels. The sidewalk feels slippery. Still, it's a good day for a walk. Anytime I think of Hazel being lost and the trees look crooked, like question marks. The trees know more than I do. Bent trees. Bent clouds. Bent sun. Where is that woman? Well, she's not here in the park. Nope. Can't see her anywhere. I'm worried. How will she survive without me? I'll check over by that strip-mall down the street. Maybe, she wandered down to the Mac's store. Look at the cars. You'd think people would stay home on a day like this. Bloody fools! I make it to the strip-mall. Lots of people here today. Besides the Mac's store, there's just a hairdressing salon, a small take-out place selling pizza by the piece, an East Indian spice store, a video rental place, a small bakery that makes rolls I would die for and of course, a small liquor store. Aw, there's Hazel in the middle of that crowd over there. I get closer. I hear her telling a truck driver a joke. Hazel never tells jokes: "Did you hear the one about the Black Baptist minister in Missouri who discovers that somebody in his church started a rumor about him belonging to the Ku Klax Klan? In church that Sunday, he asks and asks his parishioners if they know who started the rumour. Finally, the minister demands an answer. Suddenly, a gorgeous Black woman sitting in a back pew, springs to her feet and says, "I'm sorry, Minister. I only said you were a wizard under the sheets." I laugh and laugh and move closer. Then I slip on the wet parking lot and fall. Hurts. Maybe I broke something. Can't move my hip. I'm crying. Pain's so bad. Hazel's now next to me. Sirens. I feel her tears, her fingers all over my face, like small animals. "Paramedics will be here soon," I hear a man say. Sirens. Ambulance finally here.

Two paramedics slide me in, shut the doors. Hazel is crouched right beside me, fingers trembling, her cane like an exclamation mark looking for its origins. The paramedic tells me I may have broken my left hip and that they'll get me into X-ray as soon as we arrive at Emergency. "Call my son, Mark. He'll take care of things. Call my son, Mark. Hazel will be lost without me."

• • •

In the hospital, my father gurgles in his crib-like bed. He's had a small stroke on the left side of his brain. Shock. Blood supply to the brain cut off. Brain swelling. Paralysis. Loss of sensation. Difficulty in movement with one side of the body. Affects speech. He will recover but will now have to live in a place with more day-to-day care. In the midst of many hospital voices coming from the public address system, I ask "How are you today, Dad?" He mumbles and slurs, as if he has finally taken up residence in that vault of heaven and why am I taking so long to get there. Then, an awful smell permeates my father's room, and he smiles like he's contributing something to the world. I lift his sheet. J.L. needs to have his diaper changed. I find a clean diaper. I nearly die from the smell, turn my head and take a deep, hospital breath—a lesser of two evils. "Revenge of the diaper," I say to J.L.'s room-mate. I tape on a clean diaper and stuff the dirty one into a plastic bag. Then, I drop the bag into a can outside the room. After, I gently cover my father with blankets, as if he were my child, a son I don't know what to do with. He opens and closes his hands, like two tired Prayer plants – hand signals of the heart. I wish I knew what to say. I get down on my knees. The room suddenly smells fresh, clean. I easily understand my father's babbling.

• • •

When I was eight, that song about wishing upon a star was mine. Nobody knew my secret. Quivering star. A star that kept its promise, that Sunday evening star. I always wanted my parents to take care of me.

My mother ran out of places to hide her whiskey. She's tried the closet, her dresser drawers, the hamper of dirty laundry and behind the drapes. She's tried inside the back of the big radio, behind the stove, in cupboards, in winter boots, in pockets of summer jackets in the winter, in pockets of winter jackets in the summer, in the fake fireplace, and under her fur hat. You name it and she used it. I was the only one who knew every hiding place because I watched, found the bottle and poured her booze down the toilet. I had to take care of my mother. The best hiding place was her cough syrup bottle which always stayed right on the kitchen counter in full view of all of us. We all thought she was taking this medicine for her cough. She filled the bottle with rye and water and just left it right next to the bread. Nobody touched Hazel's cough syrup. Then, one day I saw her drinking straight out of the cough syrup bottle and then belting back second's and third's. "Where's your spoon, Mom?" I said. "Use your spoon."

Outside the hospital, after visiting my father, I search the brick red sky for that same star. Nothing sparkles or shines. Astronomers must be baffled, lost for new names. The sky is now a wall of bricks, the moon its bullseye centre. I will wish upon this Sunday night moon and the wish will never come true. If Peter Pan were here now, he'd be a bricklayer. I have been eight years of age for the last thirty-odd years, now forced into double digits, kicking and screaming at my world of parental duty. Honour. Pride. Love. Memory. Forgiveness. Let go. Let go. Maybe the stars are being re-shaped, re-charged. I believe. I believe. First things first. I have a job to finish.

THE HUMAN, THE HABS
AND THE HOLY BOX

TODAY A VOICE TELLS ME, "Hazel, you are made for the dying of children".

The room at the senior's lodge is warm and smells of mothballs, like a closet of winter clothes. Pink slipcovers drape the sofa chairs, the butterfly wings of my aging. The television is on low, with talk-show murmuring. Two moon-yellow bananas protrude from a green bowl on top of my television, as if they are the ears of an alien talk-show host. An African Violet, next to the bananas, is a gift of love and guilt from my daughter in New York.

Hazel, the old me, sits by herself like an etching in a far corner of a museum. J.L. is back from the hospital and is outside in the lounge reading the story of Phil Niekro, the baseball knuckleball pitcher. If my husband could, he'd live the rest of his life in a baseball dugout, that predictable half-hole in the ground. "Knuckleballs, you never know how they'll come at you. Reminds me of you," J. L. said the other day.

One of my grand-daughters, Marie, is visiting and brings me, the old one, a doll and some butter tarts as a peace offering, because of the time I lashed out at her for turning down the TV on J.L. and me. Marie also doesn't spend every moment trying to please me so I say, "You obviously bought those butter tarts for your grandpa because you know I can't eat them. Right?"

"Not true, Granny. I had no idea," Marie says. I eat just

about anything—when it suits me, which Marie doesn't have to know about right now.

"Here's where I'm working this summer, Granny." And Marie shows me a Quality Inn pamphlet. I force a smile, old wound returning to create new wounds. "Auntie and Uncle are coming from New York for Stampede, Granny. Bet you'll be glad to see them. I know I sure miss them both. We'll have some fun when they're here: Stampede Parade, Chuckwagon Races, Dancing, Stampede Breakfasts, Barbeques.

"Have a can of Orange Crush," I say.

Yesterday, my husband went to the doctor and was given a Cancer-free prognosis. I don't believe that doctor. J.L. had his prostate and testicles removed, but the doctors didn't remove everything; J.L. only pretended to have surgery. Now, J.L. uses his walker and cane to move around because of that bad hip of his. I made a deal with him. No hugs, kissing—no contact at all. Wouldn't want to catch his Cancer. And as anyone can see, we sleep in separate beds. The doctor kept saying J.L. was fine, and that it's impossible to catch his Cancer. But you never know. You never know, right?

I jump up from my chair, like a flower bursting its seeds. I turn off the television and shuffle towards Marie. I stand over her and stab the stuffy air as if I'm warming up for a trick with a dart. "You have a relationship with your grandpa. A secret relationship!" Marie's face is cracked, like a box of puzzle pieces. "You wait for him at the door whenever he comes inside. When you help him take his coat off, you are not being a granddaughter. You and your grandfather look at each other passionately!

When you and your sister were visiting your grandpa in the hospital after he broke his hip, I saw what was happening. When you helped your grandfather out of bed you pushed him right back and jumped into bed with him. Right there with all your clothes on, you had sex with him. Your legs were in the air. I saw it all! You really enjoyed yourself. Doctors, nurses and other patients in your grandfather's room pretended not to notice. Sarah saw it too but she'd never tell the truth. I know what they say about identical twins!"

Marie quakes so hard, her flesh could fall off her bones right there. Good!

"Granny, you're sick!" She sounds so much like her Uncle Jimmy who doesn't know the difference between being educated and being intelligent.

I watch Marie run out of the room and stumble down the hall. I hope she screams the sky blueless and stops the world from breathing.

I rip open Marie's doll to see if it has any babies inside. Perhaps I will find the one I lost after Mark was born.

Today I am made for the dying of children.

• • •

It's her brain, scarred with a kind of rare plaque—Alzheimer's. But it can't be just that. She's always been somewhat twisted. Played mind games with me as far back as I can remember. My brother, Jimmy, says it's because of our Irish Catholic background: girls not being as important as boys; guilt, fear, arguing, humour, talking, talking, drinking, drinking, an ego that always projects the me, me, me. I should have just stopped fighting with her and gave her the attention she needed. I shouldn't be too hard on her. She's my mother. She's sick. I turned out to be an alcoholic, just like her. I had to stop drinking because Pauline threatened to leave and I started going to those group therapy meetings. I gave up booze for Pauline but I soon discovered I did it for myself. Not long ago I heard that nearly fifty percent of all male offsprings of alcoholics become alcoholics themselves. The number of females is about thirty percent. Is it because of that never-ending genetic roulette of being male? Anyhow, after the brain reaches a certain age, it may stop growing, even revert to old behaviors. Maybe, Marie reminds my mom of someone from the past. My mother raged once because a woman phoned our house when I was a boy. My parents fought. I was really young, maybe five or six. I remember my mother snarling and waving her hand, as if she were trying to sweep a secret into a corner. I would run outside, dig for worms, tear them in half and bury them twice as deep. I couldn't stand them disagreeing, arguing, fighting. Drove me crazy actually. I still can't handle conflict very well. Hazel still says: "Don't tell your father. Don't tell your father" whenever she wants me to buy booze for her and then slips me an extra five dollar bill. J.L still talks about women he once had. Hazel pretends it is all a big joke and laughs on cue whenever my dad mentions an old girlfriend's name. Once, when I was a boy, he went to a Blind Pig, which was an after hours bar in Montreal. There, he and his buddies had a few quarts of beer with women they met. I never knew if it was before or after he married my mother. It all seemed like a joke at the time, the story. Anyhow, yesterday a counsellor said that my mother could be depressed about a number of things. Must be tough on her. I haven't heard her laugh for awhile. Then there's that antidepressant drug in England, which gives patients an uplifting bonus: When they yawn, they have an orgasm. Some of the patients who are over their depression continue taking the medication because of the side effect. In fact, one woman, who felt better after being depressed for several months, wanted to continue taking the drug forever and began to seek out the most boring men in her office, at parties and in bars. She even found she could experience an orgasm by deliberately yawning. I think the drug is called Clomipramine and five per cent of its users have the orgasm side effect. Now, I'm on the floor, laughter shaking me free. *What do they have for men? What do they have for men?*

• • •

Hazel is alone in a hotel room somewhere, long ago, and she hasn't changed clothes in a week. She smells. She's growing a new skin. Better stop drinking or I'll die. She fills her bathtub with warm water but no soap and climbs in fully clothed. The phone rings. Hazel jumps out of the tub and sloshes to the telephone. As she listens, Hazel removes her soggy clothes with one hand and they plop at her feet. It's Room Service. "Do I want that bottle of Canadian Club? Yes! Good." It will be brought to her room in a few minutes. She carries her clothes into the bathroom and drops them in a pile, like old skins. A knock at the door. Hazel is naked except for a blanket wrapped around her. She pays for the rye. Heads back to the bathtub. Opens a window. Flings all her wet clothes into the busy street below. Birds sway, change direction. A traffic cop almost chokes from the panties on his whistle when he sees Hazel's clothes descending, freezing in the winter air, anonymous. Hazel then climbs into the now-empty tub. Pours the whiskey all over herself and the blanket. Lights a match. Lights a second match. Lights a third match.

J.L. searches everywhere. Somewhere out there, Hazel is drinking in a bar. J.L. walks the streets. Checks every bar. Worries. Worries. Finds her in a lounge near the strip mall. She's perched, swaying on a bar-stool, sharing her resentments with the bartender: lousy home, lousy neighbors, husband doesn't understand, ungrateful kids. Good. At least, J.L. now knows where Hazel is. The air smells, like burnt skin. He says nothing. Turns around. Leaves. Goes back home, glad that his search was short this evening.

• • •

I shave my father's face because he no longer can do it himself. J.L. is recovering from a broken hip and he has aged faster than a fast-flipping calendar in one of those 1940's films. A metal plate binds the pieces of bone. J.L. is ready to leave the world but he'd like to do it clean-shaven.

I fill a styrofoam cup with warm water.

"Okay, dad, here goes. Remember this is my first time."

"You'll do better than me," he says.

I pat warm water on his face, and in his eyes, I see a new trust though I always felt I could do no wrong in J.L.'s eyes. The shaving cream covers brown spots, scars and colonies of black heads on his upper cheeks. Laugh lines reach down from his eyes to his side burns. I am so close, so close to the face of my father. He has one clearly defined brown eye and one watery brown and green.

Eye-brown moon and a green moon, craters. Hair fringes J.L.'s head, like a new halo. Then I begin with slow downward strokes from each of his ears. After, I glide the razor down his cheeks to his chin, back to his upper lip and then his neck. Blood from tiny cuts stain the foam, as if seeping into snow.

"Sorry about the nicks, Dad," I say.

"Don't feel a thing, Son."

I palm warm water onto his face. Use a face cloth to remove any leftover soap, blood.

"Missed a couple of spots," I say.

"Go ahead," he says blinking.

I palm more warm water on his face and use less shaving cream. Old cuts. New cuts. Plowing leftover stubble, blood, soap with the razor. I use a warm cloth to dab J.L.'s face clean and watch needle-lines of blood escape, harden.

• • •

In the hospital bed, I am wrapped in enough sheets and blankets to keep me warm in any world. I hear myself mumble that I can't feel too much in my left arm and leg. I hate my mumbling! I feel my left eyelid drooping, as if it were a miniature curtain announcing the end of a play. Moonlight is searching for something in my wide-open right eye. When I sit up and see my reflection in the window, my eye sockets are deep, hollow and clouded in black. A middle-aged nurse, who looks exactly like the head nurse in the movie, One Flew Over The Cukoo's Nest, only ten years older, enters my room and asks:

96

"What is your name, Sir? Tell me today's date. What hospital are you in? What city do you live in?"

"My name is Johnny. Today's date is Febjune the Fourth. This is... The... Hospital." "Do you know what city this is?"

Again the nurse asks the same four questions, presumably to find out if I am mentally competent.

"Leave me alone, will ya!" I shout.

The nurse apologizes, leaves. Another nurse comes into the room, and cups her hand under my head, then helps me curl into the most comfortable position, the fetal one. My order.

Moments later, I awake, and from my hospital bed, I hear my voice quivering, like a bird feathered in fear. This morning, I was downstairs getting my first therapy for the hip. When they were finished, this porter offered to wheel me back to the elevator and then to my room. Imagine, all that just for me.

The days are so long for me, I imagine myself climbing out of bed and pushing the hands of my clock forward, forward. Nights are longer, particularly when I listen to visitors talking with the other patients. I need to hear. I need the feel of words. Even from the second nurse who is tall, about the same age as the first nurse. She has an instant joy about her though, and I could pluck her out of a thousand nurses. I will never forget her.

"Looks like you had a good shave. You'll have to fight us all off," she jokes while taking my blood pressure.

I look at my crotch, at the nurse, at my groin again.

"Then what would I do?" I laugh.

"Put it on your dream agenda for tonight," she says.

"Then what would I do?"

"Pretend you still have all your parts."

"Then what would I do?" I smile, my half-green, half-brown eye winking at the moon.

• • •

I tried to scratch Golden's ears this morning, but there was deadness in my touch. Last night, I heard his exhaling again and again. When does he ever sleep? Me, I never sleep through a whole night; I don't need to. Drunks never do. Neither do dogs. I take short naps, then move around the house. I often end up on the couch. Golden doesn't get out of my way anymore. It's as if the dog found out about my secret, that I could see out of the corners of my eyes. Used to be that when I'd drag my feet towards him, he'd get up on his paws and saunter off somewhere. Simple. I don't know why everyone around here thinks Golden is so smart though. Bet he could use more dog training school. However, I miss relaxing on the couch downstairs at Mark's with Golden, especially when J.L and me were listening to Nat King Cole in the late afternoon. I' d rub and rub his chest singing along with Nat. Whenever I'd stop rubbing his chest though, Golden gave me his paw whether I wanted it or not. Then I'd continue my rubbing, chanting, chanting. I think Golden liked my voice better than Nat King Cole's. I also think Golden misses the taste of J.L.'s fingers. J.L. always wondered why Golden kissed his fingers so much. I knew it was the taste of nicotine on his hands that Golden loved; whenever J.L. went out for a smoke, he'd be out there waiting, waiting for J.L. to finish that last puff so that the dog could lick his fingers. Aw, all this sappy stuff! One night after a few too many, I got Golden back for knowing my secret. I figured out exactly how to make that dog crazy. After a few drinks, I invited Golden to the bathroom with me. He followed me and I stuck my head into the toilet. First, nothing happened and I pulled my head out. I pretended to be sick and Golden growled, running in tiny circles. I laughed and stuck my head into the toilet bowl again and again. In. Out. In. Out. The noises I made! I knew dogs' ears and noses are far more sensitive than my ears and nose. Imagine. Then, I pushed myself to my feet using the toilet and pretended to vomit all over Golden again. Always pretending over and over. Golden ran in tiny circles, faster and faster until my laughter stopped. Finally, I stood up and staggered back to

*my chair. There, I poured myself another one and rubbed
Golden's chest while singing how unforgettable I was. Too bad
I don't smoke. Too bad!*

• • •

The question is aging me. What do I do about my parents?
I wake at one a.m.. Slap the mattress with one hand, then the
other. Kick the blankets off. Can't sleep nearly every night
now. I look outside at the stars and see nothing but dull circles of yellow. I climb back into bed with the dim lights keeping my eyelids open, like bent, miniature crowbars. The ceiling. Black. White. Back out of bed.

Tiptoe to the kitchen. Guzzle orange juice straight out of the
jug, as if it were a potion, a solution. Eat chocolate fudge
cookies in a trance. Insanity: doing the same thing over and
over again and expecting different results. Juice. Cookies.
Back to bed. Up again five minutes later to the washroom. Sit
on the toilet. Do nothing. Read everything, including the back
of the toothpaste tube. Stand. No flushing required. Back to
bed. Lie on my stomach. Flip on my side with a pillow, without a pillow, with blankets, without blankets, with sheets,
without sheets. On my feet again. Two a.m. Pad to the living-
groom and pace, pace, pace. Try the couch. This way and that
way. Not long enough for my frame. Try the fetal position.

My mother told me I wasn't an easy delivery. In the dark, I
was born by Caesarean section. I appeared to be in good
health. I had two perfectly formed heads. Two hearts. Two
arms. Two stomachs. Two separate nervous systems. One was
mine, the other Hazel's. From the waist down I was a fusion
of two bodies and, the doctors said three lungs. Both of my
heads connected to the vertebrae that joined around my waist.
That's why each side of my body reacts separately to stimulus.
Each breathes independently. I am totally surrounded by dull
haloes of yellow. No part of me can sleep, and I silently beg
my parents to start me all over again.

Up on my feet again. Lie on the carpet. Spread my legs, my toes. Close my legs. Close my toes. Three a.m.. Moonlight is so expansive, so still I can cover myself with it and I do. Sleep. Sleep. Sleep. I lie there on my back, naked, pleading, pleading with my eyes too close. I pray to the moon and swear there is electricity in my brain. I turn on my stomach and grab hold of a table leg. Help me! Help me! Then I change positions so both hands can grasp a different table leg. Tick. Tick. Tick. I look up, twist my head and see the clock showing four a.m.. Back to the bedroom. Lie on my back in bed and count every possible animal I can think of. Even the sheep are desperate. The animals change size too quickly: mice, elephants, cats, horses and wolves. Backwards. Forwards. Sit on the edge of the bed, on the floor, on my knees. Beg God for just a moment of sleep. My head is warm. I am a kid again on one of those thick rope swings—God's arms supporting me, swinging me back and forth, back and forth in the sunlight. And the clock reads five a.m. Then my eyes roll so far back into my head that I'm able to dream an entire year's dreams in sixty minutes before the alarm clock rings.

• • •

It happens, like slow-motion lightning. Fatigue takes over. My body is numb. I smell a lit fuse inside my head. I'm standing over my half-filled grocery cart. Forcing myself, I push my cart to the snack-bar area where I sit down on a plastic orange bench. Immediately, my body convulses back and forth, my brain short-circuiting its electricity. All of my skin vibrates. I flip. I flop. I pass out.

I half-awake in an ambulance with a paramedic watching over me. "What happened?" I mumble.

"You had a seizure in Safeway," he says.

"Seizure... seizure... me?"

"Yes Sir. Just take it easy."

"I feel like I've been in a fight with a dozen men. I'm tired, sore everywhere!"

"That's to be expected. Your seizure was a big one. Have you been missing a lot of sleep latcly? What about missing meals?"

"That's for sure."

In the hospital's emergency ward, two doctors stand over me, one of whom is a neurologist. I awake fully. Every muscle in my body has lost a war.

"Who beat me up?" I ask.

"How are you sleeping these days? Have you been missing meals?"

Why does everyone ask the same questions?

"Just rest here awhile. We'll run some tests," says the second doctor.

"I... could... use... some... sleep," I mumble.

Then I drift off. My body remains in the emergency ward. My brain is removed and taken somewhere for examination. My heart is too tired to understand. I fall into a first time sleep since my parents came to live with us.

● ● ●

Jimmy reads to me a note from my father saying he is feeling great and that he'll pray for me. Seems that he's leaving the hospital in a couple of days. He had just gone down to the hospital's chapel and lit a candle for me in case the electricity comes back to my brain. I am given Dilantin to keep the voltage down.

Doctors peer over me, as if I'm a specimen from another world, their whispers, like houseflies, buzzing about my head. Compared to the other visitors, the doctors stand out because of their easy way of moving, their restraint, as if their hearts half-gnawed away by despair, were conserving their strength for the ordeals to come. The neurologist is not sure but he suspects the seizure may have been caused by sleep deprivation and not eating properly. For the rest of my life I'll have to take Dilantin pills daily and voluntarily give up driving for one year. Otherwise, I could end up being scraped off an express-way, like road kill. I can go home, but I'm to return to the hospital tomorrow for more tests.

I rent four videos to watch downstairs in the rumpus-room because I need to stay awake all night for tomorrow's tests. At four a.m., an apparition of Hazel bursts out of her bedroom without her white cane. She shuffles towards the washroom, arms and hands mapping their way across the walls, and she knocks an African mask off one wall. I get up but sit right down again. Hazel may be too startled and fall. I hold my breath. Hazel stops, wraps herself in her own arms and hands, as if creating a sudden shield. The warrior behind the African mask dances wildly. I block my ears from the warrior's song, lower the sound on the television, and drop my own shield. Hazel falls to one knee, feels around the floor, finds the mask, lifts it carefully to her face, feels for the nail and skillfully hangs it back on the wall, as if she'd been knocking masks off walls all her life. Finally, she grasps the bathroom door han-dle, thrusts it open and snaps on the light. When she emerges, I half-expect Hazel to notice the dull light of the TV at the other end of the rumpus room but she doesn't or perhaps, won't. I say nothing. Watch her move carefully. Listen to her whisper: "Forgive me, Mark. Forgive me, Mark." Is she really there? Hazel flicks off the bathroom light. Begins her finger-mapping back to the bedroom. When Hazel reaches her bed-room door, her hands suddenly fold themselves in prayer. Then, I hear her climbing back into bed whispering her HOLY HOLY'S, her amazon's chant. Finally, I hear her praying the paint off her favorite statue. Again.

● ● ●

The next morning, at the hospital, a technician tapes wires to my head and says, "Now just relax." Humm... beep...hummm...beep. The machine records patterns from an exhausted brain and looks for damage. After, the technician shows me strips of paper with tiny pictograms, looking like my parents, riding round and round, up and down on a miniature Merry Go Round. If I can't stop the turn-about, will I climb aboard?

Later, the blinking light test: a red, then a green light is shone through my eyes to my brain. Then, the same test, using blue and yellow spotlights. One after the other they reach my brain. Both pick up speed and I lose all sense of colour, moving so fast now that the colours mutilate each other like a sudden, fierce storm on an autumn road wiping out fallen leaves.

• • •

My house has become a minefield. Always there is a bomb ready to explode. We can only handle one at a time so conflicts are saved up, like secrets. Each potential explosion fizzles with fuses set to trick the brain. I want to detonate each on another planet peopled by emotional eununchs. My mother, Marie, my mother, Pauline, my mother, me, my father, me. I am handcuffed. More and more, I've been imagining myself out of the world I've left and not left. This inventing has me in an airforce where I'm part of a three-man crew doing fighter jet maintenance. When we're not working or fighting for sleep, we drink beer after beer from cans stacked in our lockers. One night, we are suddenly hit with a full-scale mortar attack while working on the tarmac. The night overwhelms us. Perfect targets. Two of us make it back to safety. I don't. Another explosion. Screaming. A steel-toe, blown off my boot. More screaming from my pounding head. My bloodied foot, just out of reach. The other two crewmembers rush outside and carry me on a stretcher. I faint before they reach safety.

"Pretend you're on a warm, sunny beach. You're sipping a cold one while chatting with a woman who is so so brilliant and beautiful, even the sun has to catch its breath," one of the crewmen says.

"She's a genius. She's stunning," I gasp.

"That's right," says the other crewman. "Now remember, your toes are snuggled in warm sand. You're in...heaven!"

"Then why am I losing my mind?" I ask.

"It's the beach, the sand, the beer and the woman. The world you've left and not left," says the first crewman.

I awake with my face inside out.

• • •

My parents are now in the same hospital, Hazel having surgery that might restore some vision and J.L. needs two more days of therapy for his hip; father on the Sixth Floor, mother on the Third.

When J.L. discovers that Hazel is so close, he begs me to shave him for the second time in thirty minutes, as if his face might suddenly grow a full day's beard on the elevator trip down to Hazel. "Let's get rolling!" he shouts. When we arrive in my mother's room, my parents extend their shaky fingers to each other with a code of devotion older than me. J.L. pushes himself up from his wheelchair and kisses Hazel's face with a tender awkwardness. His fingers fumble, tracing each of her facial lines, the longer and deeper the line, the more gentle he becomes, as if he's a surveyor, her face a map. Tears trickle from J.L.'s left eye only, his brown and green eye, the eye that has made him feel so self-conscious from the first moment he saw himself in a mirror. Seeing my father cry for the first time, washes me clean, makes me a newborn. "You look great!" J.L. says. "And you look edible!" An old joke between them. They paw each other, like kittens, kiss fingers, hands, wrists and faces. I leave. Let them be.

• • •

In the hospital corridor, I imagine my mother in her coffin. I want to see Hazel's body and try to feel something for her. But she's not ready yet; they still have to make up her face, do her hair, put on a new dress. I don't care. I want to see her now. Now! I want to see my mother right now! I see Hazel looking like she just came off a three-day bender. Puffy, red-lined cheeks. Red nose. Porcelain white body. Closed whiskey eyes. I run to hold her cold, cold hand. Then I force myself to feel something, anything for her. And then it happens. Hazel's hand becomes warmer, warmer.

• • •

All sins are related to fear somehow. Some are like insects running crazily, stinging the walls of my heart and head. I'm tired of the same sins being committed over and over. I keep going back to feel the same pain. Absurd. I'm afraid to have Hazel and J.L. stay here any longer because we'll destroy each other. Don't blame yourself. And I'm afraid that if I put them in a senior's home, they won't be taken care of properly. Don't blame yourself for that either. Yes, I know but feelings have no logic. Let's get back to my father and his sins against that poor, poor me. The one image I have of my father is of a gentle-spirited man who really only thought about himself and nobody else. I see the same Shriner's Circus poster on a telephone pole every year inviting kids to the Montreal Forum and wishing I could go. I never did. I just wanted someone to take care of me sometimes. That's all. And I think J.L. knew about my mother and me when I was a boy but he was afraid of her, afraid to say anything. After that sixteen-year-old boy sexually abused me when I was little, I told my parents but they didn't do anything about it, except tell me to stay away from that older kid. J.L.'s only sin against me was not having a backbone sometimes. Like me. I come by it honestly. Maybe I'll have to let go of my parents. How? Let them have their own lives. You know what you have to do. Think progress rather than perfection. Yea, sure. Progress. Perfection. Have you ever put yourself in your parents' shoes? Have you ever once thought about how they felt? Why should I? Why should I?

• • •

At the front door, I see two pairs of shoes that I thought were no longer here. One is a pair of tan-colored loafers, my mother calls her walking shoes; they lean inward, are odorless and scuffed at the toes; Hazel's shoes point in the same direction—straight ahead. The dark brown Oxfords which my father wears everywhere, are in need of a shine. They look and smell as if they are rotting inside. They are bent and wrinkled in the middle and one shoelace is frayed and shorter than the other. The toes are turned upward towards the moon, almost like a pair of clown shoes. My father's shoes are pointed in this and that direction.

• • •

Trying my mother's shoes on for size, I find I am a girl in a house of four sisters and two brothers. Even though I try so hard, I do not fit in anywhere. Although I don't like groups, I join the church choir because I love to sing. I also love swimming, water. I go to Mass at least twice a week because I'm afraid of going straight to Hell. Every morning, I practice being a good girl by smiling in the bathroom mirror. In my house I'm almost ignored because I'm a girl; my brothers are more important because they will be men. Why does that have to happen?

Something's wrong here. I am always afraid. Afraid I won't have any friends. Afraid I won't have enough money. Afraid of the God I know and don't know. I never feel at ease. Everyone makes me angry so easily too, and I never forget the harm done to me. Wrath is my middle name. The lump in my stomach keeps growing because good girls can't show anger. "Have a little drink of rye and ginger ale," my oldest sister, Jean, says at a party one night. Right away, I feel better. I sneak another one in the kitchen. And that's it! I'm back in the party singing songs for my aunts and uncles. The more songs

I sing, the more sips they give me from their drinks. I can now fit in anywhere. Anywhere. Why be afraid? If I get annoyed, I can always "drink at" that person; that'll fix 'em!

• • •

Wearing my father's shoes, I find myself in a house with one sister and five brothers. Gentle kid. I feel so different from my brothers and sister; when they want something, they take it. They know it all—especially my older brother, Leroy and my kid brother, Frank. I love baseball and tennis and I'm pretty good at playing both. I don't know the difference between a hammer and a saw but I don't care. I go as far as Grade Ten in school but I want to go to medical school, use my hands to fix people. I try different jobs, usually low-paying clerical jobs. Canadian Vickers, the railway for thirty years and Beggi Cruise Lines. I also did some volunteer work, driving guys younger than me to medical appointments.

Did you know that I have one brown eye and one brown and green eye? Must be God's way of reminding me that I'm not allowed to be very good at anything. Everyone knows my colours.

• • •

J.L. is ready to leave the hospital, but I'll have to stay a few days longer because my Hazel eyes need more healing. Oh, there's Mark. He looks like he's going to leap out of his skin. He tells us we can't live with him anymore. We're driving him crazy. Ha, we've had to tiptoe around on eggshells since Day One. And that precious stereo of his, well his music doesn't exactly blow up my skirts. Never has. Listen to him; the entire world revolves around what he sees, how he feels. Ever since we moved in, I've felt this horrible sensation in my chest, as if I'd swallowed a lump of something that would not go up or down, like a piece of hard turnip or a chunk of raw carrot. He can't handle us. He can't handle us. Poor, poor baby! There he goes running off and telling J.L. to get someone else to wheel him back to his room. Poor, poor Mark! Get me a shot of rye, will ya! And while you're at it, get that son of mine a baby bottle of warm milk.

• • •

One time in a dream of mine, J.L. and I worked part-time as upholsterers. We were re-doing J.L.'s sofa chair in the living room. J.L. does absolutely nothing except hand me the staple-gun when I call for it. I get so drunk that I place little Mark inside and staple everything up. Mark cries from inside the chair. Think. Think. I hear a voice. J.L. and I search everywhere for Mark. I panic. Take another shot of rye. Mark's voice is here and there. Then I hear his breathing near the sofa chair. I rip the cloth off, as if raping the sofa chair. There are staples in my hands; they tear at my skin like tiny needles. I scoop Mark out faster than whiskey goes down my throat. I cry, cry in Mark's hair. I gulp rye straight out of the bottle. Once. Twice. Mark smiles in my arms and taps on my whiskey bottle. I watch J.L. lower, then shake his head and take the staple-gun away.

• • •

I see Mark, his bare hands. His knuckles. We have to leave. Shaking, Mark drives downtown to The Kirby Center. His hands break on the steering wheel. He drives through a red light but other drivers sense his insanity; they swerve and miss a collision. Get a grip on yourself, Mark! Get a grip!

The Kirby Center psychologist has probably heard Mark's story a hundred times before, and she'll tell him that he's lasted far longer than most people. Yea, sure, lady, sure, but we're not most people! I hear her telling Mark that it's an impossible situation, that on rare occasions, it works if "the woman of the house" is submissive with her own mother. There is nothing said about "the man of the house" and his mother. Nothing! I keep hearing the word, "unhealthy". Unhealthy. Unhealthy. I imagine hundreds of files in an open filing cabinet, all cases like ours—Manila coffins in a steel drawer.

• • •

Oh so long ago, J.L.'s mother stayed with us for three weeks when Mark was a young boy. I couldn't wait until she left. She had taken over, like a boss I once had in a factory job who made us all feel like moronic plebeians. And she even broke my favorite lamp, not by accident. No matter how many times I had it repaired, the lamp never worked again. I'm still angry about that lamp.

Walls crumble. My words fit together like a two-piece puzzle suddenly connected. All heart. No sense. It's what my family does in the tightening hold of emotional investment. Finally, I am able to talk with Mark about our six month stay. We both agree, for the first time ever: We can't stay much longer. The silence has been a long, long blade, knifing, knifing. Walls and walls of avoidance.

I hear J.L. say to Mark in a voice as light as a robin's feather, we're looking into a nursing home and we'll be moving out soon. Meals will be prepared for us. We'll be with people our own age. Please don't be angry, Mark but we have to wait until February First instead of January First. And then Mark saying in a deadened monotone, "It doesn't matter, now, Dad. As long as you know you and Mom have to leave, for everyone's sake."

I finally see Mark as having been hooked up to one thing or another since the day he was born. Addicted to addictions. Like me. On the eve of my death, I will be sober, needing morphine to kill the last hours of my pain. I will say, Please let me die completely clean and sober. Do you hear me? Cancel the morphine!

• • •

At the bank, I'm signing my name over and over to prove I am my parent's son, as if my only identity is in a pen. Next, I show two pieces of identification, including my license; and the bank agrees that I am me. I realize the signing power I now have for Hazel, for J.L.. After I sign my name three more times, I become someone else, someone who has ceased resenting. Mother sloshing in her liquids. Father in his oceans of avoidance. Me clinging to the garden I hope to grow, earth with more clay than anything else. I have the sudden knowledge of being a son who has feet made of putty. Just like his parents. Across a screen in my head, the letters of my first name, M A R K are writing themselves over and over, even after I leave the bank. Each letter is a step forward, backward, forward, as if the alphabet were reinventing itself. The letters of my last name are a long line of pleas for forgiveness. "Your signature will protect your parents and their money," the bank clerk said. The protector is a new man no longer caked with soil, and I have not met him before today. The man now signs his name with such grace, as if he were looping thread with an index finger. Yes, I am my parents' son. For too long, my signature has belonged to a man who grinded down his bottom teeth in his sleep until they became crooked nails, a man whose name I never knew.

• • •

They are away, not away, still in the hospital but soon to be released. Mark and I work fast in the -38 C. cold. We move our parents' possessions out of Mark's house to the senior's home. Mark always says that the only exercise I get is when my skin crawls during a horror movie, but today I can tell he is surprised by my vigor. I even pack their dust in boxes along with pictures of Jesus Christ, a St. Anthony statue and a plaque depicting the Twelve Stations of The Cross; all in one big cardboard box,

Hazel's holy box. We leave this box until last, like a final glass plea on my mother's rosary. On top of the luggage rack, my father's stuffed chair is tied down with yellow wax rope. Inside are bulging boxes and sagging green garbage bags. Mark and I stuff the station-wagon full, make our first trip, drive through the creaky, cold morning to the senior's home.

Inside, we hear tiny bursts of curious but polite whispers coming from the dining room as we walk by, arms full of mother's and father's possessions. It's as if we are actually carrying our parents instead of boxes along a parade route lined with gray heads, white heads and wheelchairs, wheelchairs, wheelchairs. We move fast. Unload. Move quickly. Unload. Move faster to warm up. "One more load, " I say to Mark.

Back home, we tie my mother's stuffed chair to the luggage rack, bared to the frigid sky. I see Hazel now, with a tumbler of rye in hand, sitting in her chair, proud of her huge fur coat that smells of mothballs, and she too is held down with yellow rope, like a late Christmas gift. *Great view up here up here, she says. Know something, boys? Lighten up, will ya! Life's too short to be small. Know what I mean?*

"Hey, Jimmy, we could be in a Marx Brother's film with you being Harpo sliding an enormous harp across a stage as big as a parking-lot," Mark suggests.

"And you could be Groucho prancing and chasing women around Hazel's empty chair," I say.

"Hey, Harpo, I know what really makes people attractive. Some people keep saying that it's what's upstairs that counts. Well, I have something upstairs. My ... ."

"You better drive this time, Mark."

The tires move like blocks of ice. When we arrive with our last load, I leave the holy box on the front seat, and we untie my mother's chair. Mark picks up the holy box, as if it contains the story of his life, and it sags in his arms. "Damn box," I hear Mark mutter, frost forming on his green ski jacket. We should leave it out in the cold by that trash bin. Even the thick dust abruptly puffs into the cold air, like the ashes from a last cigar.

• • •

The night after the move, I am eight years old again. Although Hazel doesn't know the difference between an oar and a raft and couldn't care less, we are in a rowboat together. We glide out to the middle of a lake in a place called Miles Isles. Except for us, the lake is empty. I stand up in the boat and begin counting a thousand islands that are not there. An invisible hand pushes me over into the water, and the last sound I hear is laughter. I am drowning, drowning in fright. Suddenly, I feel a hand reaching through the water and grabbing me by my T-shirt, yanking me out of the lake and into the boat, as if I was a minnow in a trap. "That was very STU-PID of you to stand up in the boat!" Hazel says. *Then, she is alone in another boat on a dark lake with no oars, no motor, no sail, no anchor. I hear her talking about an old boyfriend: That guy was so handsome I could have eaten his face. Helluva lot tastier than Digestive Cookies and tea. But he was mean. Each time I didn't like what he said, he'd tell me my face belonged on the bottom of a lake with the other Catfish. Mean. But long on looks. And all I wanted to do was, well you know... wish upon his star!*

• • •

It's Spring. After six months in my house, they'll soon leave the hospital to live in the senior's home. Pauline and I slip downstairs to the empty bedroom, as if we are two kids ready to open presents. No mother praying. No father snoring. Even their smells are gone. We strip. Taste each other. Fall into my mother's bed. We make love, make love, tongues road-mapping each other from head-to-toe and back again, surveyors of passion. We take turns calling out cities we still want to visit, then carve their geographies on each other: Cairo, Dublin, Vienna, Rome. Cairo, Dublin, Vienna, Rome. A chant. Then Cairo and Dublin. Cairo and Vienna. "Cairo, you'll never be the same," Pauline says. Then I swear I hear my mother praying for me. *Yes, God, that Mark is still the man of the house. Please keep him that way. Please, God! He's my man, God. My man. Please give him all the strength he needs. He and I can always have a little nap together if he gets too tired, God. You know, just like we did when he was a boy.*

I stop making love. I have found a city I do not want to visit, a decrepit city filled with corpses. Maggots under my skin. Pauline leaves me alone. She knows. She... knows.

That night I lie on my mother's bed but I am restless, unable to sleep, Can she still be here? Is this another one of her bad whiskey jokes? In a far corner of the room, I see a bottle cap from a booze bottle. Hazel's voice is trapped inside, an echo from a small cave. I slide off her bed and slip into my moccasin slippers. It's after midnight. I wheeze my way upstairs. New Cold. Old virus. Cough syrup washes a Tylenol down my throat. With a suppressed cough, I tiptoe into my bedroom and wake Pauline with my Cold noises.

"Couldn't sleep down there, eh?" she mumbles half-awake.

"Miss you," I say.

And we make love, in our own bed.

●　●　●

It's my first night in the nursing home. The new hip feels better and I'm not bedridden anymore. Just gotta use that cane and sometimes the walker. Chains, cords, buttons, switches. God, I'm so scared. So tired. Need someone, anyone. Pull the cord. A small orange light. Looks like a drunkard's nose. And a nurse bounds into the room, big as a barn door. "Did you call?" she asks. Now why would I want a nurse? Just tried to find the light switch. "Don't pull the chain unless you need me, she says. When you pull it, you pull my chain." Is she kidding? Sorry, I say and my voice still sounds lumpy. I'm doped up, not sleepy. She leaves, in a scratchy-scritchy turn of starched skirts. I'll get her. One of my sons will help.

When Jimmy comes to visit, I ask him to pull the chain and then hide in the closet. He does, you bet, and when Nursey comes back, huffing like a steam engine, she says, "You pulled the chain again. You're pulling my chain!" Impossible. Can't she see that I've been standing by the window with my cane, getting ready to pull the curtains closed? Bet if she had eyes in back of her head, it still wouldn't help her know what's really going on. Maybe your chain's not working, Nursey. "I'll go back and check the main board", she says. Go ahead Nursey. Go right ahead. I tell Jimmy to pull the cord again. And Nursey comes stomping into my room. "There was somebody pulling the chain!" Didn't she see that I was in the bathroom all the time. Nobody's pulling your chain, Nursey. Maybe, it's the wiring. Go check. Okay, go for it, Jimmy! This will really get Nursey going. She chugs back into my room, like an old boat. "MY CHAIN! MY CHAIN! WILL YOU PLEASE STOP PULLING MY CHAIN UNLESS YOU REALLY NEED ME! I'd never pull your chain, Nursey. You work too hard. Can't she see that I'm trying to get some sleep. Nursey, Nursey, nobody here but me. I've been under the covers all the time.

• • •

Sometimes, I cannot pull myself up from my bed because my body feels like it belongs to a sumo wrestler. Hazel comes across and visits me all the time but she can't lift and turn me when the nurse is busy so they attach a steel, movable bar to the bed frame. Now, I'm supposed to pull myself up from the pillow and then to my feet. I practice once, twice, three times, and then I do it, but I'm angry because nobody helps me. "You have to do it on your own," Jimmy says. I know. I know but I don't want to do it all on my own anymore. That Jimmy, he's always so right, just like a member of one of those service clubs. Anyhow, I can't stand alone and look outside anymore, so why bother. Every tree I think of is now crooked. Hazel says I should bring the outside in, but I need the fresh air, even though Hazel says she will leave my window open all the time. We can't leave this place unless accompanied by someone. Besides, this is the most comfortable bed I've ever had in my life. When I was twenty, I had to sleep on my mother's couch for a few weeks when my older brother Leroy moved back home. Although I wasn't the youngest or oldest of my four brothers and one sister, I could never understand why I had to sleep on that couch. I remember waking one morning and couldn't get up, my back hurt so bad. I was sore for weeks until Leroy moved out again to get married. Seems like I never left my mother's couch until I moved into this senior's home. I know. I know. You've heard this before. But, I'm allowed to repeat myself!

I could honestly die in this bed.

• • •

Like an X and an O, my grandparents now live diagonally across the hall from each other. Separate names on different doors. Separate rooms. They always meet in front of Grandma's room to go to the dining room together; they shuffle through thickets of wheelchairs to meals. Or, they meet in Grandpa's room for TV, to receive telephone calls from family.

I'm playing a pretend GO FISH with Hazel, her first card game in years, I'm sure. She claps her hands. Grandma's as small and frail as a wounded chickadee. She's heavily rouged. She wears a helmet of curls, the same colour as my hair, and it shines like the wood of the chair she's perched upon. Her yellow pantsuit clings to her legs, droops at the shoulders. She hums a song that sounds like How Much Is That Doggie In The Window, but the rasp of her voice makes me think of climbing a rope to the sky, where someone can make sure we'll all be saved, one day. Her teeth are rotten, breath foul. And my dad says, "I want you to see a dentist."

"Naw, the smell of old can't be fixed," Hazel says. "I'm not worried so you shouldn't be either." GO FISH! GO!

And I can see my dad, a boy digging in the dirt, burrowing through topsoil, scooping out holes; he buries empty bottles in the backyard. Even today, my dad's always up to his elbows in soil, dirt.

"You should read a good mystery," Grandma tells me. "Try one Marie, if you really want to know about death."

GO FISH, Granny, GO FISH.

And she's swinging her broom again like a sword, to chase away bullies, but the weapon is aimed at my dad when she catches him burying her unopened bottles of rye.

I'm still afraid of her.

"It would help if we could at least SEE her fuse getting shorter," my father said the other day.

When I leave I don't know whether to salute or click my heels, like Dorothy in The Wizard Of Oz.

• • •

Where does a mother go to say goodbye to her son? Mark has been kind this evening; he has set up our TV, radio, taught me how to move the "ON-OFF" knobs. But where do I go?

It's the first time in months I've been able to look at Mark since that day between Marie and me. Feels like I'm in a sunny, peaceful meadow that smells of fresh grass and daisies. Mark is here visiting and J.L. is having a nap. One of my eyes is half-closed and the colour has drained away. My face feels contorted and must look like the side of a hill after a severe rainstorm. My other eye is wide-open, a valley. I want Mark back, wish I hadn't lost him so long ago. "Forgive me," I say. "Forgive me." Then my fingers stroke Mark's face lightly, as if it were the rarest of all silks. I write letters on his palms. I honestly have never known how to love him because his anger kept pushing me away. "Was it anything I did? Something I said?" I say. Then it happens. The roar of a jet splits the sky in half. He won't tell me it was my drinking, how one minute I'm telling him that he's the strongest, most handsome man of the house and in my next breath telling him to go to Hell. No, he won't. He probably thinks I don't remember. When the jet noise has subsided, my son and I look at each other. He knows.

"The night is as black as I've ever seen it," Mark says. "Except for a few streetlights, three stars and the moon."

I want to say, sorry if I loved you too hard but I still do, and the words print themselves on the black of my sky.

"I hope the move out of your house doesn't mean goodbye forever," I say.

"Don't worry about it, Hazel," he says.

"Well, it sure wasn't easy for all of us living together."

"It's just you and me, Mom. We don't fit. Never could figure it out."

"You know, you've been pushing me away from the day you were born."

"Why do you keep saying that? Makes me crazy!"

"Do I look or sound like a mother who would make her son crazy?"

• • •

On the front page of tomorrow's newspaper, there will be a photograph of my mother and me, and the caption will say that there's no such day as yesterday.

All this time she waited, thinking she was long past surgery for her eyes because a Montreal doctor had told Hazel she was too old, that she should join the Canadian National Institute for the Blind. Just a few days ago, a Calgary doctor operated on both of her eyes and restored most vision in one of them. Nothing could be done with the other eye, and my mother said she wanted to throw it away, like a sin from her past. Now she can see a tree outside her window for the first time in years; if she smiled any harder, her grin would make a full circle.

"Let's try out your vision on the hockey game, Mom," I say

flicking on the television. "if you can see players' sticks like you can that tree, you're on your way."

"Sure, let's try it," she says.

The game is crucial. If The Habs win, the Stanley Cup goes to Montreal. If they lose, the series goes to a seventh game in Los Angeles.

"Remember, Hazel, watch the sticks!"

"I can already see them. A couple of them, including Gretzky's, seem to be made of aluminum."

"That's right, Mom."

The announcer continues: *Le Clair to DiPietro. DiPietro slips across the blueline. Fakes a shot. He shoots. He scores! One to nothing for Montreal.* I hold up one finger, like an exclamation mark to my mother's face. "How many, Hazel?"

"One," she says.

Carson to Robitallle. Robitaille to McSorley. Back to Robitaille. He shoots. He scores What a shot by Robitaille! I hold a finger up from each of my two hands. "Hazel, how many fingers?"

"Two."

"Good!"

Odelein to Damphousse. Damphousse to Muller. Muller shoots. Hits the post. Shoots again. A scramble in front of the net. He scores! "What do you see now, Mom? How many fingers?"

"I see nothing but my son making me laugh."

LeCaire to Keane. Keane shoots. Rebound to Lebeau. Lebeau waits. Shoots. Scores!

I hold up three fingers from one hand and stick out my tongue at Hazel.

"Three!"

The game moves on, and finally, Montreal wins by a score of 4-1. Patrick Roy, the Montreal goaltender, is over to one side, away from the Stanley Cup. Like an offering to my mother, he holds his wooden stick up to the camera. Then I remember the wooden cross I once wore around my neck, a miniature cross Hazel gave me. The cross was handmade by a priest. Altar boys brought him discarded, broken hockey sticks from rinks everywhere. I can't recall how I lost that cross.

• • •

At the picnic table, away from Hazel booze and Mark whining, I watch the going down of the Sunday sun. Huge, white throngs of people make their way to the horizon where they will slowly bleed to death on fences. I rub my right ear. Scratch my nose. Nothing but slow breathing sliding through my Sunday. Blurred. Obscured. Darkened. Disguised. Concealed. A sky burnt by days.

I like being called J.L.; Johnny sounds like a gangster's name. "J.L., J.L." I say it over and over and my blurred name wraps my Sunday in ribbons of sun. Pauline told me yesterday that I carry myself as carefully as if I were handling a full glass of ginger ale: even, steady, careful not to spill it. Listen to the age of my ginger ale name. Yes, it is true. I am old for so much longer than I am young.

Awake, I dream of baseball games: scooping grounders out of the dirt at shortstop, throwing runners out at first base with an arm of steel and afterwards, wolfing down two hot dogs smothered in mustard, relish and raw onions and a regular Coke; none of that Diet or Caffeine-Free stuff. I am an unknown hero in a documentary about eating at a baseball game. You must hear my life story.

Big Band music: I'm humming In The Mood along with the music and I remember when I first saw that same band perform live in Montreal. I thought the bandleader closed his eyes while playing the trombone because he must be reading the swarm of musical notes on the insides of his eyelids. Watch the darkness, you'll burn yourself on the horizon!

Maurice "The Rocket" Richard, and the Montréal Canadiens: I'd skip work and allow Mark and Jimmy to miss a day of school just so we could go see another one of those Stanley Cup parades. Les Canadiens sont là toujours! Grinning, waving heroes. Shrines floating down St. Catherine street. Hazy fanatics. In my blood. In my blood. Disguised day. Chocolate fudge. Lemon meringue pies. Don't worry boys, I'll tell your teachers you had dentist appointments.

Those movies with that family of brothers were perfect. But, on second thought, (only my opinion of course) they seemed too small in number for me. Maybe, they could have used more members, like an authentic black sheep brother and perhaps one of those administrative-type, older sisters who held the act together with a comic, iron fist. Concealed laughter bursting at the seams of light. If you don't laugh soon, your underwear will shatter, shatter.

I keep reinventing events from memories so I can make Hazel and Mark go away. Telephone poles grow taller; tiny springs hang from each pole, like steel muscles, my muscles. Remaining lines of sunlight tie up my brown eye and my brown and green eye, swirling, swirling. When will you let me know when I'm good at something, God? Are you bemused, absorbed with others at the moment? When? I can cook hamburger. I can make fudge. I make people laugh. Do those count? Do they? A blue and white eye watches me clean the kitchen and fold up the horizon and God for the day. Again. Let me help you pack, Hazel. Let me help you pack, Mark.

On a black-lined coloring book page, I use thick crayons. I colour in a half-hidden horse brown, a cow black, a pig pink, a rooster red and even Old MacDonald himself. The farm doesn't belong to him anymore. Not to Mark or Hazel. Not to anyone. I want Old MacDonald's farm but I wouldn't be handy enough around the place. I colour him gray on the shoulders of Mark and Hazel, on the shoulders of my idea of God.

• • •

I didn't know Mark was watching me in the backyard last
Sunday. "You looked like you invented the sad daydreamer,"
he said. This Sunday afternoon Mark takes me for Coke and
doughnuts. Then we drive to the river and rest on what has
become our bench overlooking the Bow River. Normally, I sit
on the west end of my bench and Mark on the east—the water
always flows in the same direction, west to east—but today
we've traded places. At my back, city traffic whizzes by, leaving me contentedly behind. Rollerblades, bikers, and joggers
suddenly become mute when they pass us, like noise turned
inside-out. The Bow glides under the sun with a silent, slow-
motioned grace. I feel its pull, the ripples, like reaching arms,
one at a time. The river's song calms our heartbeats. My son.
Yes, he's with me, one arm around my shoulder. "I love you,
Dad", Mark says. It's that simple. Mark has no idea how much
I love him, never has, though it began the day he was born,
when I threw my hat, high, down the hospital corridor in St.
Mary's hospital in Montreal. A son. I had a son! The river only
flows in one direction.

Above our heads, poplar leaves, shimmer and turn, stirred
by a new, cautious wind.

• • •

I'm in the front seat of the car, ready to go to our Sunday
afternoon mecca of doughnuts and Coke. Hazel sits in the back
seat, head down, hands folded like a choirgirl's. With all doors
shut, the acrid smell of my urine claws its way through my
nose. Even with the window rolled down, my lungs are desperate for fresh air. Hazel says nothing, just smiles and studies
her gathered hands. Mark knew this might happen and, he
covered my seat with a green garbage bag. I notice the added
protection, even though he thinks I don't. Wind pulls the urine
odour through my open window, as if the car were being

cleansed of an infection. As the last whiff lingers, I'm brought back to the Montreal Forum, which didn't include Hazel.

Mark and I are witnessing the Habs thrash the Toronto Maple Leafs while Hazel is at home with her Agatha Christie book and rye. At the end of the First Period, I lead Mark to the men's washroom. Inside, I smell nothing but urine, moth balls and stale beer. All the men wear long coats and fedora hats. They stand at the urinals, like cartoon characters in MEN ONLY magazines. When it is Mark's turn, he finds he cannot pee standing so close to the strange man beside him. He turns his head and looks to me for help but I just smile and wave a hand at him. After The Second Period, Mark tells me he really needs to go pee and we head down to the men's washroom again. He tries to pee at the urinal. Nothing. Then he tries a stall. Nothing. Five minutes into the Third Period, Mark has an accident in his pants and cries with shame. I console him and wrap my long coat around him. When we get home, Mark pees enough urine to flood the Montreal Forum. I tell him the peeing was an accident, and to have a good sleep. Now, I look at Mark and tell him not to worry. It's only pee. It's my pants. A urinal wouldn't have helped. Neither would a stall. Or a trip home.

"At least now you're wearing a man-sized diaper," he says. That sounds nice, son, but the pee smell is returning, stronger than ever, and I have nowhere to go.

• • •

At the doughnut shop, it's my turn to pay and I hesitate, as if hoarding a pot of gold beneath gathering clouds at the end of the world's only rainbow. "I'll pay... again, Dad. Don't worry about it," Mark says. I do this with restaurant tips too. I never recovered from the Great Depression of the 1930's. After studying my nickel-and-dime tip a few weeks ago, I heard the waitress say, "I would rather you left me nothing at all." So that's what I did. It drives Mark crazy, but what the hell does he know about being really broke? Mark always expected me to earn a bigger salary and he never understood that I don't write my own paycheck.

Last night, I dreamt I was sentenced to five years probation and ordered to reimburse a bank more than three thousand dollars. When the bank machine would not give me any money, I pulled out a thirty-eight and fired six shots into the machine. The story is on the six o'clock news and Hazel tapes it for the family. The only times she shows the tape is when relatives come to visit. After a few drinks, she teaches everyone how to get something for nothing. "It's easy," she slurs. "Just...eh... watch J.L.." A cousin tells Hazel that if she wants to fool the family, she ought to act fooled herself.

Now, on another Tim Horton's afternoon, Hazel dips deeply into her purse, her fingers retrieving handfuls of silver and fans it onto the table for Mark.

"Hazel, I'll pay," Mark says. He's such a good boy.

"No! No! No!. Take what it costs from all of this," she insists.

"It's all right, Hazel. Let Mark pay today." Then I scoop up the silver and drop it all into Hazel's coat pocket. Her face scrunches up. She turns to Mark with a look that says she has nothing to do with all of this. Then Hazel grins, as if the money were a fast deposit in her own pot at the other end of the rainbow. Meanwhile, Mark pays again through gritted teeth and his face is so red-hot it could melt the icing off my chocolate doughnut.

Outside, the sky loses some of its colours and looks like the underside of a mackerel.

There's Mark and I on another Sunday, in Tim Horton's, eating chocolate doughnuts, like two athletes at a pre-game meal. When I listen to myself talk about the Montreal Canadiens, my words are filled with the absolute red, white and blue paintstrokes and my eyes swell with water. If it'll make you feel better, I'll pay for our doughnuts, today, Mark.

I haven't seen the Habs play like that since the mid-late 1970's. Exciting. Lots of energy. Speed. Vincent Damphousse.

Kirk Muller. Even Brain Bellows. And Denis Savard making opposing defensemen sweat and turn into red, white and blue knots with those curly Q's of his. Just beautiful! Wheeling. Floating. Finesse. Deking. That swirl of colours flooding the opponent's blue line. Drives those defensemen crazy. Makes them tremble so hard, their numbers almost fall off. Blur. Crisscrossing. A rainbow beauty! He shoots. He scores! I once played a game at the Montreal Forum. Played for the railway. Got so wrapped up, I honestly felt that the Habs were on the ice too. I couldn't handle it. Scored on my own goalie. Maybe, I was wearing a Habs uniform, carried a Hab's stick. Did I ever get teased by anyone and everyone! I didn't care. It was like playing in a holy place, a real holy hockey place!

I remember those animal acts on The Ed Sullivan Show. My eyes would look like they were crying and my mouth would be wide-open, as if we were at a live circus. I know the kids were always curious about the water in my eyes because they used to ask me why elephants and dogs doing tricks made me cry. I was just... excited, that's all. Same thing when we watched comedy movies together. Also, I wonder if the kids ever noticed that I always turned my head to see if they were enjoying everything as much as me; if they were, my eyes would get wetter.

To tell the truth, the water helped me forget about my brown eye and my brown and green eye. How I always wanted to have the same coloured eyes!

Oh, Oh, there it is again. My eyes are getting all wet again. I'm nervous. My voice crumbles, like my last chocolate dough-nut did. Someone from the Calgary Cannons baseball team phoned me yesterday. The man said he knew I was a real baseball fan, that I once played shortstop. He even described how my left hand was like a magic wand digging grounders out of the dirt and firing 'em waist-high to the first baseman. Coaches used to shake their heads and ask me why I didn't go past semi-pro ball. "You've got natural talent! You're major league material," they used to say. Why should I believe them?

Right? By the way, how did that Cannons manager know I was a southpaw? Bet someone called the Calgary Cannons office, right? No? Nobody did? Then, how come the man knew so much about me and baseball? Imagine, someone from our Triple "A" baseball team taking the time to phone ME.

Now, outside Tim Horton's, a bus pulls up, and the entire Calgary Cannons baseball team pours into the doughnut shop. Every player is wearing his game uniform. The team manager approaches me and presents me with A Golden Glove, making my eyes nearly slip into a watery grave for the first time ever. The rest of the team surrounds our table and applauds, as if I were some kind of superstar being inducted into the Baseball Hall of Fame. How did they know? How did you find out about me and baseball? "You're our man!" says the manager. Everyone in Tim Horton's stands on chairs, tables and the countertop, spoons rattling on coffee cups and cheering so loudly that I swear all the doughnuts become tiny piles of crumbs, as if the entire world knows how I believed I'd never be good at anything.

• • •

I just can't find my make-up bag and I've been searching, searching for hours, days, weeks, months, my whole stinking life. I'm sure I put it on the top shelf of my closet, between the folds of my Hudson's Bay blanket. Not there. I've taken it down a million times and shook it out, like a magician's scarf. Not in the bathroom on the shelf next to my toothpowder, dammit and not in my denture cup, dammit, not behind the toilet, dammit, not in the tub, not in the damn tissue box, not even in the garbage can.

I feel my face burning. Hot! Hot! Where's that pillow of mine? I shake out the pillow. Slam! Slam! To hell with my bed! I whack my pillow on the headboard. On the night table. Shit, I knocked that glass of water over. The lamp shade's had it. I slam the wall, and the painting of a serene farmer's field J.L.

and I received for a wedding present, spins around its nail like a square wheel. There are feathers everywhere. I feel like I'm in a glass globe filled with snowflakes. Once, Mark gave me one like it. I remember fighting over a broken toy, glass shards under my unsteady feet. Money. Rye. Money. Rum. Money. Vodka. I watch Mark riding his bike to school, into the wind, his chestnut hair, so like mine, blowing straight back, always into the wild wind. I pray. I pray for strength to make it through the wall of wind, pray, as if God were a compassionate weatherman. And on his ride home from school, the wind at his back, and he hardly has to pedal, but still I pray. Just in case. No money. Never enough rye, rum, vodka. Eleven hundred dollars saved up, hidden in my make-up bag for just in case so nobody and nothing can turn us upside down again. Something to be thankful for this day. But I just can't find it!

• • •

On Thanksgiving, we celebrate in Mark's house, our family circle squared, everyone in his or her corner, as always. In my corner, I scarcely breathe, tentative as a canary, the money-case secreted in my bosom, its strings twisted like my mind. I want to apologize to Marie, say I'm sorry for that other woman from forty years ago, not this one all dressed up in her Thanksgiving best and perched in a rocking chair. Sorry. Sorry. A chattering word. It arrives with a show of intense love and departs with a knife in someone's back. Sorry. Sorry. Sorry. Make amends. Means that I plan to change. Over there, in another corner, Jimmy and his wife argue about their daughter's ballet lessons. Duelling. Duelling. Their way of showing affection, I suppose. I've always watched Jimmy walking his own family's tightrope, Now he sags, like an unplayed accordian.

Come on Jimmy, do something will you! You behave like somebody with no thoughts around you—are you afraid of your own wife or something! In his corner, J.L. smiles, happy to have us all together, as if he's in a family magazine or movie. His gray eyebrows are like that brush I use to unclog the bathroom sink. When he sneezes, J. L. lifts half the people in this room out of their seats. J.L. will die from a swollen, soggy heart. Yesterday, he offered to swap hearts with me so he could carry all our pain to the grave. Mark's dog, Golden, runs back and forth, licking everyone's fingers, his corner empty. He's learned the value of boredom now, like an old hit-and-run-lover. Sarah must be glad we're gone, no more being quiet for us. On the piano bench, her legs curl around each other, like bashful giraffe necks. Her eyebrows rise and fall, as if emphasizing each note on the music sheet. Her shoulders turn inward. She's on a mission of sorts, so Sarah's fingers seem to explode on the keys. Sometimes she misses a note and her hands seem to become impatient, nothing stops her from playing, though nobody is listening. There directly above the sheet music is a photograph of Sarah in front of the Moulin Rouge in Paris. She told me it helps her concentrate on playing her best. Beethoven's Fifth. Her fingers have lives of their own. She doesn't have to outguess her Granny's moods anymore. Mark says Sarah has a heart bigger than this or any piano.

• • •

In a nearby room, I play my favourite Marie song on my flute, a broken song. The door is open. Everyone listens to my Thanksgiving song, Joy to the World. It was always Granny's most requested song. My toes massage each other; my fingers have simple intentions. Their mixtures are measured from elements found in the walls of my heart. Simple. One false start. A second. My dad says I was born with enough character to carry me around the world three times. Searching for the ceiling my eyes glare, like spotlights. Third start. I sing the first three notes, then play the entire song with a slow flight towards that place of joy. When the song is over, the joy is replaced by a person I swear I'll never be. There he or she is, another alcoholic in the family, another drunk's genes waiting to be passed on, like a family card game of sorts.

There I will be, years from now, playing flute in a band. At least that's how it begins. I get better and better. Join a bigger band. I don't see my parents much because now I'm on the road a lot and Mom has to run their new boardinghouse in Calgary. Dad's blood is partially filled with a quart of Molson's Export Ale. Anyhow, our first job is a dump of a hotel in Le Pas. And on from there, we play all the bars. Lots of booze. Lots of messing around with other men, even though I'd recently married the bass player in our band. My new husband thinks we have a marriage made in heaven but I always figure out a way to slip away every few days to be in the arms of another man, usually another guy from the band. Later on, my mother is in the audience sipping rye and water when we play a bar back home in Calgary. She definitely knows something's wrong with me; she left all her boarders alone, for the first time ever, to check up on me. Well, by this time, I'm playing in my fifth band, one of the best in western Canada. I am so drunk on stage that I sing off key, play my flute off key. The band stops playing, as if the roof just caved in. I continue. My mother climbs up on the stage at the intermission. I get fired. My husband yanks the wedding ring off my finger, nearly takes a knuckle with it and then stuffs his wedding band down the front of my jeans. "Know what you can do with that ring, eh!" he shouts.

"Still have room in my boarding-house," my mother says to me. "Come for some Thanksgiving turkey."

• • •

Ah, hell, I gave the make-up bag to Marie. She can use the money for university. Hurts too much. I can't take the pain anymore, the fright, the rage. Last week, a woman from one of those groups told me I'd end up in a nuthouse or six feet under if I kept on drinking and I told her to go preach in a toilet bowl. But the woman was right. I've tried hospitals, detox centres, and those meetings. All I heard was: "Meetings saved my life. These meetings showed me how to live. I'm so grateful for those meetings." I want to escape, jump out of my skin. Go live in someone else. Quickly. Before I'm trapped inside me forever. Listen to that Jimmy, whining that I should keep my money; he probably just wants it for himself. And Mark, telling everyone that I can do what I want with my money; he sounds like some kind of hero; used to pull the same stunt after watching the Lone Ranger on TV when he was a boy. Now there's Jimmy's wife, trying to sound so clever by telling everyone over and over that she has nothing to say. Now, Pauline is shouting that I can spend my money any way I want; she never ever shouts and this side of her belongs to a stranger. J.L. just keeps saying that the money belongs to both of us. Everyone in this room is crazy! Listen to them. I'm tired of it all. I'm so, so sorry for what I said to Marie. Wish I had a damn knife to end it all. Maybe a few pills. Naww! I'd be the laughing stock of the family. They'd say I didn't have the guts to kill myself, or else I didn't even have the brains to do it properly. Yeah, that's what they'd say. Will you people please shut up! Leave Marie and my money alone!. That's right, I gave her my make-up bag of money. Please! Please! Please forgive me, Marie! Never mind what everyone's saying! There's Marie coming towards me again, the money-bag sticking out of her pocket, like a rolled-up flag belonging to no country. Maybe she could hide it in my holy box until she needs it. I feel better for the first time in months. And I do not... take a drink.

• • •

Outside my house, I discover a mound of rose petals on the sidewalk. None of the petals have been flattened or crushed by feet. I stop, check to see if anyone is looking and remove my running shoes. I bury my toes in the roses. I feel the cool, soft, sweet-smelling, red skins, as innocent as children clinging to a mother. The rose petals adhere to my toes, like the thin, loving fingertips of a God that is now mine too. Hazel and I don't see God in the same way, but that doesn't matter. We're all looking for God, anyway. I like my way. It works. Simple. No incense. No holy holy's. No clutter. No ranting priest or minister on a sweltering summer day reminding us that if we think it's hot here, imagine how hot it is in Hell. No once-a-week God. I don't have to go out of my way to express sadness and joy.

"We all need ranting. Makes us listen!" I hear Hazel say.

"You have your way. I have mine."

"I heard that Mark. God will get you for this!"

"I'm sure He will, Hazel. I'm sure He will."

I smell the roses under my skin.

• • •

I have to do it. So many have tried to talk the anger out of me so I can see why my love for you has been worn away to naked bone. Even a writer friend has offered an ode to me in his latest book hoping the song would push any mother love past my teeth. I hear it. I hear it. But the words have been locked in my throat so many times that my mouth is raw from all the telling I was going to do. I love you. I love you.

Here in a room of delicate bright lines, I measure my breathing against yours. I trace the long, narrow marks on your face and they barely open and close to my touch. Some lines reach up and down, like tiny magic wands. They show me how clearly I have fooled myself, how much blinder than anyone I have been, all of this caused by twisted tricks of the heart and head. Other lines are your arms reaching, reaching for me from that first day I refused to sit on your knee. Still others lead to the small, nowhere places where I still hide. Your half-open, colourless eye belongs to that eternal child who is me. Watch me. Watch me cry the blindness out. Catch my tears in your skirt, like wet leaves from an October poplar tree. What was that? I'm still welcome to sit on your knee? Here, sit on mine. I promise not to throw you to the floor and push me back into myself.

Perhaps we should have been physically blind together. Maybe I would not have remembered, falsely or otherwise, those distorted, mother and son moments, still smelling like fresh blood and urine. And those other marks on your face are the bars of a prison cell, now softened to allow you out and me in. Here, lay your head on my shoulder. Let me massage your forehead. Smoothen you. Smoothen me. Close your holy eyes. Breathe me back to life. You're on my knee . We're in a rocking chair. Can you hear it? Listen. I'm humming my anger to sleep. Forever sleep. Please listen. Listen to my rock-a-bye, rock-a-bye love.

• • •

On Christmas Day, we visit my parents hoping to bring Hazel back for turkey dinner. J.L. is bed-ridden and the guilt of having to leave him there alone is as thick as his mattress, although the nurse says not to worry.

"How about a shave with my new electric razor?" J.L. mumbles through a no-teeth mouth.

"I'll have to turn your bed and slide it over to the outlet so the cord can reach your face," I say.

Then, gently cupping his head, I begin the careful grinding of stubble into dust, the humming of machine on near-bone.

"I love you, Dad," I say with a voice so soft, even the razor lowers its noise, as if razors had souls.

"I love you too, Son," J.L. says, his eyelids moving like tiny, slow motion fans.

Then I start.

"Where's your girlfriend today? She must be here somewhere," I laugh.

"She only shows up AFTER my son has given me a close, close shave."

"You mean she won't kiss THAT FACE of yours unless it's clean?"

"Well you know, she's a very independent woman. Last week I took her to a movie and she ate all the popcorn. She's always hungry."

Behind me, my mother laughs along with the girls, as if the simplicity of love could only be measured in happy sounds. I look over my shoulder at Hazel and she pretends to be filling her face with popcorn.

I look back at my father and his eyes water up like two heart pools. I finish the shave and bring J.L.'s hands to his face.

"Feel this, Dad. Feel your face."

"Beautiful. Just beautiful," he breathes across his gums.

"Your girlfriend...she like dat?" I tease.

"Sometimes. She better or I never try to eat popcorn with her again."

Then J.L. turns his head sideways so he can see everyone through the silver bars of his bed. His eyes water up. Water down. I stroke the bristles of his white-haired fringe. Warm straw. Kiss the top of his head, as if I were covering him with words that make me want to catch my breath. Study the brown blotches leading, like spilt chocolate drops, to all those father places behind his eyes. Feel his eyes reach up, up and hug me down to son-size.

• • •

Big breaths. Swords. Little breaths. Daggers. Sudden. Slow. I stroke J.L.'s head. Hear breathing gone wild, as if my father's body was a lover almost done. I kiss his trembling forehead. Taste near-death. Listen to his heart reaching, reaching for sun one last time. Jimmy and I are an audience of two. Because J.L. loves to tease, we wait for his final prank. We fully expect him to suddenly sit up and laugh the skin off the face of Death.

"Come over here, boys. Have a good look down this well. Follow the plumb line. That's right. Straight to the bottom. Watch the faces."

We both look. See faces of certain family members staring back up at us. There's that uncle face, wrinkled, mean, oldest brother, who had cars and a cottage long before my father could even afford a second-hand car, who flaunted everything in front of my parents, who J.L. once said was the loneliest face in the world. The next face belongs to J.L.'s kid brother who is still alive and living inside a California beer bottle; my father's face is stone after trying everything to make his brother laugh. Then there is the face of my mother and J.L. makes his own face rigid one moment and loose and friendly the next; my father does it so quickly that his face threatens to fall off from all the exertion. After, I see Jimmy's face and it knows exactly where its eyes, nose and mouth belong but it desperately wants J.L. to just be its daddy. My big sister's face lives elsewhere, through no fault of its own, and looks exactly like a real heart. Finally, I see my own face; it doesn't fit into any family and its lines turn back on themselves, like scattered knitting needles.

Gasp. Gasping. J.L. hasn't opened an eye. Is he saving his vision for after he dies? Thump. Thumping. Paramedics burst into the room.

"You'll all have to wait outside," one says.

I take my mother for a walk down the hall. None of us are allowed to witness the thrusting, the injections straight into J.L.'s heart, the oxygen. An ancient, hunched-over woman in a nightie, whose face looks like a bowl of white thread, stares straight through me with a look that dares me to think she'll die someday. We turn and move back to the room just as the paramedics are wheeling my father's body out to the ambulance.

"Is he gone, Mark? Has he passed away?" Hazel asks.

"Just about. His heart's stopped. The paramedics are breathing for him," I say.

"He'd never let someone breathe for him. I'd better tell those guys, Mark."

"No, Mom. You better not."

But the paramedics are already out the front door.

"Didn't you hear me? Stop breathing for my husband!"

"Take her inside. I'll go with Dad to the hospital," Jimmy says.

At the hospital, J.L. is officially declared dead, as if only a hospital could tell when life was gone.

I stay with Hazel. In her room, she walks in tiny circles—little lost gusts of wind. As I stroke her very bony back, my own tears refuse to fall, like random musical notes trying to compose a song. Hazel climbs into bed; she is on a mission of sorts.

"I'm going to the hospital," I say.

"Are you dressed warm enough?" is all Hazel says.

At the hospital, I'm led into a small room where my father's corpse feels colder than the outside temperature. A thick, green tube protrudes from his mouth, like the stalk of a headless plant from the last garden I planted. His left eye, his brown and green eye, is still mostly open, as if he were making a last request to have that mysterious eyeball removed once and for all, as if it were a brown and green planet that had mistakenly fallen into J.L.'s solar system.

"My daddy's dead. My daddy's dead!" My eyes flood, burn with tears.

At the partially open doorway, a young doctor, with his back to me, waves everyone away from the room, as if he were directing traffic somewhere, somewhere. Tears stream down my face so fast, I am drowning and the salt stings my skin, like acid. I taste the pain; it wants to be felt, seen and heard. Now. I fall to my knees. Dad. I've always called him Dad. Never Daddy. Never. Daddy.

• • •

Burnt. My father has been cremated wearing a white, button-down, dress-shirt of mine. Dark suit and tie loaned to J.L.'s
body by Jimmy are returned to my brother. J.L. had few decent
clothes to die in; it would be the last thing on his mind. I
could never see me ever wearing the white shirt again anyway. My chest on J.L.'s chest. Son heart on father heart. Son
neck on father neck. Arms. Back. Stomach. Everything but the
act of buttoning.

Two hours to go from cold flesh to hot ash when the oven
has been already working for awhile. Four hours, if the body
is the first one of the day. J.L.'s is the first on New Year's morning, 1998. There is a black, Vincent smile under the word:
IMPRESSIONISTS on my new calendar, as if Van Gogh were
smiling a new night for the occasion. Above the January days
and numbers is the picture of a painting from Vincent Van
Gogh entitled: Imperial Crown Fritillaria in a Copper Vase.
Copper. The metal of my father's urn. Orange and yellow
perennials are in full bloom except for three, who pretend to
sag with eyes as sad as twilight, but are really slinking under
the dark towards sun. Bulbous plants of the lily family nod-
ding their bell-shaped heads at the Van Gogh, speckled darkness, their leaves sifting through my father's four-hour ashes
and re-creating the white button-down, dress-shirt I used to
wear, like a gray puzzle.

*In Africa today, a newspaper says a popular taxi driver who
used an old Mercedes-Benz sedan for most of his thirty-year
career, is dead. Relatives decide to honour him by burying him
in a coffin replica of his vehicle which includes windshield
wipers, rearview and side-view mirrors (with real glass), an
antenna (taken from a radio), a Mercedes-Benz emblem on
the hood, exhaust pipe, reflectors and license plates. And the
car-maker says that the deceased may have been poor in life
but when he dies, no more poverty. In the taxidriver's coffin,
his needs for the spirit world will be met with porcelain bowls
overflowing with cotton, numerous bars of soap, sponges,
razors, talcum powder, camphor balls, a plastic drinking cup,*

a spoon, a white cotton T-shirt and two large pieces of fabric. If he wants a cup of tea, he has a cup. If he wants cocoa, he has a spoon. If he wants to look good, he can comb his hair. This is a celebration. And I imagine J.L. buried in a coffin replica of his second-hand Corvair with everything he'll ever want in an enormous box of chocolates or fudge, munching, munching in that sweet tooth spirit world of his.

Ashes. My father now weighing about seven pounds as I carry him around the house. Pauline takes two photographs of me holding the urn to my chest. Daddy. Daddy. She says my sweater may be too dark and there won't be enough contrast. I hold the urn higher, higher till it rests on my shoulder and watch its copper face stare back at me from the bathroom mirror. I see and hear J.L. shaving and sneezing that almost apologetic sneeze of his. The soap. The brush. It wakes me too early every school morning, nearly shakes Jimmy and me out of our beds. That annoying father sound I'd love to hear one more time. *Wake me, Daddy. Wake me.* Then I see my father in his sleeveless undershirt patting his face with warm water when the shaving is done. He sneezes again. Again. Like muffled sounds of shotgun blasts. Sorry. Sorry. Six a.m. noises from an apologetic father heart.

At the cemetery, the outside temperature is minus thirty degrees Celsius. The priest says his words with gloveless hands and reminds us not to worry because he's an old Saskatchewan farm boy. The urn is slipped into the grave but topples over. I jump in feet-first and set the urn straight, as if it were the only road sign left on earth.

"Now you all know where to go when you need to say goodbye," Hazel says as she falls to her knees and kisses the frozen ground.

• • •

I am a sober angel. Here at the foot of my bed, Mark tries to comfort me. Don't worry, Mark, I am a sober angel. Has your father really gone? Has he? That J.L. was such a handsome man. A good husband. Gentle. Sure could make me laugh too. Wrap me up, Mark. I need more blankets. Leave my golden wings uncovered though. I am a sober angel, your guardian. Wear me like a gold pin on your lapel, Mark. Do you like the way my golden hands are folded over my heart? Notice the three moons on my angel hat. I look after those who are alone, Son. You love me? I know you do. Same with me. Did you know you're more handsome than anyone? How old did you say you were? Just turned fifty? No way. Mark, I want J.L. in my arms. Now. Can I join him? Can I? I am a sober angel. Is there a place in a sober heaven for me? Feels like J.L. is on his way already. Can you smell his after-shave coming from up there and over there? Should I get ready? How do I look? Angel. Spirit. Am I getting pale yet? Saint. Cherub! Please touch my wings, Mark. Touch them. Read the message they will carve when I swoop down over the Bow River. And I'll do it all from your lapel. But, you have to look up, Mark. I am a sober angel.

AGMV Marquis

MEMBER OF SCABRINI MEDIA

Quebec, Canada
2004